HAPPY

HAPPY

A NOVEL

CELINA BALJEET BASRA

^

ASTRA
HOUSE
NEW
YORK

Astra House
A Division of Astra Publishing House
astrahouse.com
Printed in the United States of America

Library of Congress Cataloging-in-Publication Data

Names: Baljeet Basra, Celina, 1986- author.
Title: Happy : a novel / by Celina Baljeet Basra.
Description: First edition. I New York : Astra House, [2023] I
Summary: "For fans of Vikas Swarup and Charles Yu, the story of a starry-eyed cinephile who leaves his rural village in Punjab to pursue his dreams-a formally daring debut novel set against the global migration crisis"--Provided by publisher.
Identifiers: LCCN 2023016040 I ISBN 9781662602306 (hardback) I ISBN 9781662602313 (ebook)
Subjects: LCGFT: Bildungsromans. I Novels.
Classification: LCC PR9110.9.B35 H37 2023 I
DDC 823/.92--dc23/eng/20230530
LC record available at https://lccn.loc.gov/2023016040

First edition

10 9 8 7 6 5 4 3 2 1

Design by Richard Oriolo
The text is set in Trade Gothic LTStd.
The titles are set in ITC Franklin Gothic Std Demi.

For Nila and Björn

What does it mean, to live in a room? Is to live in
a space to take possession of it? What does taking
possession of a place truly mean? As from when
does somewhere become truly yours? Is it
when you've put three pairs of socks to soak in a
pink plastic bowl? Is it when you've heated up
your spaghetti over a camping-gaz?

—George Perec, *Species of Spaces* (1974)

PROLOGUE

I am Happy. Happy Singh Soni.

A Punjabi currently based in Italy, I am working full-time on Europe's largest radish farm.

I am well experienced in all tasks related to radish farming: i.e., sowing radish seeds, transplanting radish sprouts, tending to the growing plants, injecting weed killers most expertly, spraying to death the ugly ones and caring for the beauties. By eradicating all uncertainty, the harvest is bountiful, always.

First and foremost, my labor is a labor of love.

I feel confident that I have reached a level of excellence in European radish farming. Hence, I want to widen my skill set and actively seek new challenges by exploring other aspects of farming in Italy. This is why I am applying for the open position as a shepherd on the island of Sardinia.

Also, I have to admit, my back would thank me if I were able to work in an upright position once more. The constant kneeling amidst the radish patches is killing my spine. I often catch myself these days musing among the vegetables, stretching my back, unable to recall who I am. For a brief moment, I exist in a blank space: a white cube smelling of lemony cleaning agent. Time expands and contracts. I pull myself back into reality by looking at my hands, greenhouse dirt underneath surprisingly rosy fingernails. The sight of my skin roots me. Brown skin with tiny pink injuries from tiny radish shovels.

What are the long-term effects of constant spine bending? Is spinelessness the desirable state after all?

I am empathic, flexible, and resilient. The journey from India, crossing deserts, mountains, walking through a vast forest I cannot name, and arriving via boat in Bari, certainly did take its toll. However, I am still alive, and I am at your service, or rather at the service of your black Sardinian sheep, pecore nere.

I can drive a tractor and a truck. I have never taken a taxi in my life, nor have I boarded a plane. I am excitable and impatient, charismatic, and single-minded. I anticipate, always. I look ahead. I identify the problem before you even know you have one. I am perpetually hungry, and I always need a snack. I miss pakoras. I miss my morning tea. I miss my mother. I tend to suffer from diarrhea more often than from constipation. My metabolism is as fast as my mind. By jumping two steps ahead, I tend to fall back three, ending up behind the starting line. But I always get back on that horse, as one should. Though I cannot ride a horse; I've only ever ridden a camel—once, at a fair, and I threw up right after. I am a Hypersensitive Introverted Extrovert. I did a test online. My love language is Words of Affirmation. I did that test, too. Most of the workers here are Sikhs like me, but, still, it tends to get lonely. I cannot say that I am happy, but I am lucky to be here, in Europe.

Strictly speaking, and I don't want to beat around the bush, my status of residency is not legal. Illegal? You may very well say so, but I couldn't possibly comment. I am currently in between nationalities, but I am certainly doing my part for the European people: providing them with the cheapest, crunchiest, reddest, and raddest radishes, bulbous and disproportionately huge, to be chopped up into European salads and to decorate European sandwiches. Let's forget about the taste for a moment, watery, carrying a faint sharpness, just a memory of its ancestor radish's sapid glory: earthy and spicy, delicate in flavor. According to my research, radishes were domesticated in Asia prior to Roman times, growing happily for a long time in what is now China, Myanmar, Vietnam, and India.

I admit, I care too much. On a frosty night in spring, I was caught sleeping with the fledgling radish sprouts, covering them in Indian scarves and blankets. Some might say I cross boundaries; I say I am passionate about my job. Leave your emotions at home? I say bring them to the workplace. That's the only way to get the job done. Crying is fine. People who cry at work are better workers, always. Those are the workers you want.

Before I came to Europe, I dreamt of Europe.

In my dreams, I envisioned my European home. German engineers, Danish designers, and Swiss cesspool specialists had joined forces to design this dream house, located in the center of Europe, somewhere pastoral and green. Out front stood a tree, an oak, with a trunk as wide as a healthy German man is tall, six feet, coincidentally, the same diameter of a Russian gas pipeline, just as sturdy and unyielding. On the crown of the tree, Dutch maidens with heart-shaped mouths were lounging, lazily spinning cotton candy out of their super long, golden hair while shitting grated gouda cheese directly into my mouth. The cheese production was as natural to them as breathing; there was nothing ugly about it. And I was standing underneath them with my mouth wide open, enjoying every morsel. The cotton candy clouds descended, hovering briefly, then covered my head like a golden veil. I was a bride, a cotton candy bride of Europe, well-fed on gouda in preparation for the wedding ceremony. Finally, the Dutch maidens turned into Dutch boys, who were frying up artisanal bacon. Somehow, they'd managed to bring state-of-the-art pans and tiny gas cookers up into the tree—

I digress. Let's just say, my foolishness is past. The dream was just a dream; radish is my reality. And I always dig where I stand.

If you were to inquire about my language skills, you'd be surprised to learn that, in addition to my ever-improving Italian, I speak a little bit of French. I taught myself back in India while watching Godard movies on my mobile phone.

My extensive experience with farm animals big and small, i.e., water buffaloes and Beetal goats, will enable me to handle the job of managing your pecore nere with ease and vigor. I am no stranger to loneliness and isolation, which will come in handy while working on those Sardinian hills alone. I will have my black sheep to keep me company.

If you would like to call my former employer as a reference, I would kindly ask: please don't. They are ignorant of my wish to widen my skill set. The coordinators don't forget and they don't forgive a debt, ever. Take my word for it; I will be the best worker you ever hire.

Do let me know if there is anything else I could send to support my application, i.e., letters of recommendation, or writing samples, such as a nine-page screenplay entitled *The Sad Dancer* (Tawa Press, 2004). I do not presently have my certificates and qualifications with me, but I am happy to ask my mother to send them from India.

I look forward to hearing from you.

Thank you for your time.

Sincerely,

Happy Singh Soni

PART ONE

WONDERLAND, JALANDHAR

Ü

WELCOME TO WONDERLAND

Welcome to Wonderland!

Yes, you heard right: an exhilarating universe of fun and leisure is now just outside your door.

Close by the flourishing cosmopolitan city of Jalandhar, less than a 25-minute drive from its bustling city center, a plethora of amusement rides and a myriad of attractions await you. Wonderland, spanning a huge 11 acres, offers Complete Fun packages to people of all age groups and unlimited ways to experience Pure Exuberance and Joy. Forget about your chores for a day and simply walk on sunshine.

Take your pleasure seriously! Become a true citizen of Wonderland! Don't hesitate; book your ticket now. We'll have you jumping for joy in no time.

Feel free to contact us if you have any questions or concerns, or to obtain information on ticket fees. We are happy to assist you, ensuring that you have the very best experience. Please note that all water rides are closed during the winter season. Please also note that people measuring over 1.98 meters tall are not allowed on most of the rides. We thank you for your understanding.

THE PRINCE OF CABBAGE LAND

The cabbage fields were the old world. The grounds of what is now Wonderland were once covered in cabbage heads. Soft green with a purple-blue tinge, neatly arranged on the ground like a bed of roses planted by a benevolent giant. As a little boy, I watched the cabbage heads rise, expand, and grow, like balls of roti dough. I even slept among them, squished in between the rows, having rolled into a wooly scarf cocoon. I was dreaming of becoming a cabbage myself. Happy Singh Soni, Prince of Cabbage Land.

On the last day of the cabbage fields, the day of the harvest of our winter cabbage, I took my cup of tea outside, squatting by the old grounds. It was brutally early. My lashes were still sticky from sleep, but the cold air was rubbing my skin awake. The fog had begun to lift just now, reluctantly. I watched the pickers prepare, knives sharpened, cabbage pouches waiting, the ancient tractor running, emitting the scent of diesel and anticipation.

Rajeev, our Picker in Chief, was also sipping tea, leaning against a broken mower. Back then, the buildings of our farm had been grouped around a square of ochre dust, lined by discarded farm machines. When I first learned how to write, I had christened it the Soni Square, painting a sign on a piece of cardboard torn from a package my brother Fatehpal had sent from Germany, filled with Royal Dansk Butter Cookies, Nivea cream, and a fancy suede jacket. I fixed the sign to a broom handle that I then stuck into the earth. Naming things could make them mine; this much I had understood by the age of six.

A dog barked in his sleep. The wild dogs of our village were yellow and slender, shuffling their long limbs into cool corners, perpetually dreaming—except for dusk and dawn, when they were wide awake and anxious. Whenever I slept among the cabbages, my mother, Gul, would come out every hour to check on me. She feared I would be gnawed on by the wild dogs, who were rumored to chew off babies' noses. Truthfully, they were rather benevolent and lazy, their criminal activities limited to stealing fresh batches of barfi left to cool under the canopy by the outdoor stove.

That morning, my father, Babbu, was up early as usual. He was walking around the compound with his youngest granddaughter in his arms, showing her the crows. Together they followed the birds' trail slowly, gently. Babbu lured them with crumbs of stale rotis. The girl cried out: *Kan*. *Crow* had been her first word. My sister Ambika had named her Amanjot. A face like a raw petal encountering the sun for the first time. She would probably go on to live in America one day, a life in the burbs with beautiful children of her own. You can already see it in some newborns, that they will be the ones to tread on solid ground. With others, already in their first breath you can feel that the earth beneath their feet will always be collapsing.

The air vibrated with the resistant huffles and shuffles of a lawn tractor. Our neighbor Satish was attempting to conquer the tall grass around his rapeseed field, long neglected. His father had died months ago, and the prodigal son had deigned to return from Delhi only after much toil and trouble. He'd been working in a mobile phone shop but acted like he'd renounced the presidency of India to return home. Seated on the tractor, he looked like a cartoon figure on a futile quest.

The motor kept dying. The tractor wasn't happy to be resurrected; he didn't want this new life, he wanted the old one, and the old one was gone forever. Finally, the tractor pushed forward with a jump, running straight into an array of rocks and gravel by the field. The tractor's motor emitted one last howl and remained mute forever. Satish stumbled onto the ground, muttering to himself, and threw one of his Bata flip-flops against the body of the silent machine, who felt nothing in return.

I'd run into Satish at that final meeting with Wonderland, Inc.; he'd been clutching a faux leather folder, sweating profusely. I had never liked him—not since he'd called me a pansy and "accidentally" poured his midmorning milk onto my crotch in preschool—but I understood why he had sold the rapeseed farm against his mother's wishes. The offer had been too wondrous to withstand. Our cabbage farm hadn't made a profit in ages. We should have switched to broccoli or lychee when we still had the chance. Cabbage, it appeared, was distinctly out of style. Wonderland, meanwhile, in a planning stage bold and hopeful, was already looking for staff. All the youth of our village had applied for the various open positions: Chief of Boating, Chief of Security, Front of House, Secretary, Safety Officer, Wellness Officer, and Lifeguard.

I had applied, too. The questions on the application form had been "fun":

Why are you an asset to Wonderland?
I am a creative, flexible multitasker, a keen adventurist, and a full-on people person. Imagination is my line of business. Pleasure is yours. I feel we are kindred spirits.

How would you describe yourself?
The Punjabi Sami Frey. Watch this space. Good things will happen soon.

If you were an object, which one would you be? And why?
I would be a tawa. Without a tawa, rotis would never rise beyond cold dough. Second thing I would be (though I know you didn't ask, and I know it isn't an object per se) is ghee—butter eases and unites, connecting opposing elements. The great harmonizer, you could call it. That is me in a nutshell.

Describe yourself in three words.
Empathic, flexible, resilient.
(This I googled, and all the above are excellent characteristics to name in an interview.)

Picture the following situation: a little girl has fallen off the swan boats. What do you do?
I would call out to someone who can swim because I, sadly, cannot. I have never seen the ocean. The well behind the house isn't deep enough to learn swimming in, although my brother Davinder tried to teach me. In the meantime, I would fashion a rescue rope out of my shirt and trousers, if need be—creativity is one of my strong suits, and I believe in the power of invention.

Where do you see yourself in five years?
In Europe, writing at a window overlooking the snow-coated Alps at dawn, the coast of Capri when the sun is high, and

the Paris skyline at dusk; a room with a most magnificent view that I can call my own. I will have sugar rotis for breakfast, lunch, and dinner, except for the days when I'll have buttery aloo paratha, having reached international stardom and total all-around happiness. My family will reside in a mansion in my garden, featuring a small cabbage field as an homage to our Punjabi home, and my father will keep two pet crows called Sweety and Pie.

HAPPY SINGH SONI—CV

Born in 1991 in Punjab, India. Writer, researcher, publisher, and aspiring actor.

Enthusiastic, ~~hungry~~ people person with leadership potential.

WORK EXPERIENCE:

1999–2008 SONI FARM
goat and cabbage care, and more
I take pride in having assisted my father in tending to the Beetal goats from an early age. The job entails discouraging the goats from jumping over the creek and frolicking in our neighbor's pastures, a task I completed mostly with great success, except for that one time they escaped to the neighboring rapeseed field and we almost lost young Hum to the tires of a tractor, which taught me to keep calm in a crisis. I learned to take the animals seriously as companion species, and to humor

them if necessary, all while firmly establishing my role as leader of the herd. Shortly, I became an expert at balancing charm and authority.

Cabbages were my close companions ever since I was a small boy—they don't call me Prince of Cabbage Land for nothing. When I touch their leaves, I can feel cabbage feels, think cabbage thoughts: black, bug, shoot, root, glib, skin, hard, want, earth, bulge, snout, sky, hole, air, wisp, gold, hold, snug, tuck, vein, crawl, mush, hot, be. Add Cabbage to my list of foreign languages. Also, I am the purveyor of a recipe for excellent, crispy cabbage pakoras, honed to perfection by generations of Sonis.

2003–2008 MR. TULI'S STATIONERY SHOP
seasonal shop assistant and paper advisor
From sorting writing paper according to color to dusting shelves and taking inventory of triangle rulers, I made myself useful across all areas of the stationery business, except handling the cashier's desk, as I am not a numbers person, but "a true people person" (Mr. Tuli). Showing great talent as a buyer, I assisted Mr. Tuli in making the paper orders for the coming season. I took great pleasure in keeping the shop's selection up-to-date with the contemporary paper market. I am happy to report Mr. Tuli is now well stocked in papers of all colors of the rainbow. Furthermore, I started an independent publishing press. Tawa Press would be flourishing by now had Mr. Tuli not have discovered said clandestine business in the back of his shop. Anything revolutionary typically starts

as a secret undertaking, and I do hope you give me credit for audacity.

2004–2005 SONI LIGHTING
lighting intern of remarkable energy
While shadowing renowned electrician and light technician Davinder Singh Soni on his comprehensive lighting renovation project in Chandigarh (i.e., Neelam Cinema and University of Chandigarh), not only did I learn about the art of lighting, becoming proficient in a great variety of lightbulbs and cables, but I was able to experience large-scale repairs and renovations in a Modernist environment. This taught me that all buildings crumble if you do not tend to them, no matter how Modernist they are.

2006–2008 HAPPY TV
director, actor, producer
The advent of YouTube brought a myriad of artistic possibilities and global broadcasting opportunities. My independent channel, Happy TV, documents everyday life around the village, including food content, bird sound, dance (you can do it, too!), philosophy, and short interviews. I am the director, producer, and main protagonist. Subscribe to my channel!

2001–2008 SCREENWRITER
self-employed (Tawa Press)
Selected titles: *Sugar Rotis for Breakfast* (2001), *Letters to Kiran* (2001–2007), *The Sad Dancer* (2004), *My Winter of Wonder* (2005), *A Thousand Light Bulbs and a Kiss* (2006),

The Dead Goats Society (2007), *Portrait Of Europe as a Young Woman* (2008), *The Children of Limca and Gul* (2008, unfinished), *Venus as a Punjabi Boy* (draft)

LANGUAGE SKILLS:
Punjabi (mother tongue)
Hindi (excellent, fluent)
English (excellent, fluent)
French (intermediary, with regards to vocabulary used in the movies of Mr. Jean-Luc Godard)
Italian (very much beginner's level)

AN INCOMPLETE LIST
OF WONDERLAND RIDES
AND ATTRACTIONS

GONNA FLY NOW

You are Rocky, running up the steps of the Philadelphia Museum of Art. Take in the view, then take an unforgettable picture! Bound to get you tons of likes on the socials. The popularity of Rocky movies and Sylvester Stallone in Punjab has remained strong since the 1980s. Is it Sly's melancholic lazy eye that likens him to a Bollywood hero? His working-class Italian heritage that makes him a king of the Punjabis' hearts? Be a hero, just for a day. Now, go on. Fly!

SWITZERLAND!

This ride reflects Bollywood's historic fascination with the central European country; Switzerland's mountains have frequently been used as a setting and backdrop for movies and more. Who doesn't remember the iconic dance sequences of the hit romance *Chandni* (1989)? SWITZERLAND! is characterized by an extraordinary slowness, and excellent scenery, populated by locals eying you warily. Expect breathtaking views, crystal-clear air, and a smashing fondue experience at Lake Zürich: chocolate, Gruyère, and more cheese the further you go. Polish up your French, Italian, and German skills (no one will reply if you mumble your apologies in English or Punjabi); reset your clocks and exchange your bills, cause we are going to SWITZERLAND!

THE PARTITION TRAIN

Refers to a particularly gruesome chapter in Indian history: the Partition in 1947, following India's independence. Flee from Punjab (India) to Punjab (Pakistan) and vice versa in this breathtaking journey by train across a country divided. Plundering mobs are waiting for you. Which route will you choose in order to survive? A suspenseful thriller of a ride, at the end of which you'll find your true home!

MILK A REAL WATER BUFFALO

Milk a real water buffalo now that farms are swiftly becoming obsolete! Yes, you heard me. Real water buffaloes! *But I've seen water buffaloes before*, you say. *At home*. Well, won't be long before they disappear entirely from the face of Punjab's earth. Buffaloes, and cows, too, are already at stake in other countries around the world.

Milk alternatives are killing them slowly. So help a water buffalo keep her job; milk her! You can even keep the milk, a bottle of our very own brand, Wonderland Buffalo Latte. (Maximum one bottle per person.)

CHATURANGA

Chess has its roots in the ancient Indian board game chaturanga. We've unearthed the rules of this long-lost pastime and magnified a chaturanga playboard to bring the game to life. Are you a Raja, Mantri, Ratha, or Gaja? Learn the rules and choose your role. Will you bring victory and glory to your country? Or will you die in combat? Let's see, shall we? ;-)

CHAMPS-ÉLYSÉES (CURRENTLY UNDER CONSTRUCTION)*

Oh, Champs-Élysées . . . oh, Champs-Élysées . . . Sing along to the well-known tune as you promenade the streets of Paris, a.k.a. the City of Love. Experience Parisian style! Croissants! Baguettes! Cigarettes! Existentialism! Revolution! France! Yes: Vive la France!

We provide authentic backdrops for your selfies and will soon offer complete wedding packages, too.

*Children under the age of 5 are currently not allowed into the Champs-Élysées for safety reasons. We thank you for your understanding.

HAPPY SINGH SONI, WONDERLAND ASSISTANT

There are many things named Wonderland: Alice's Wonderland, of course, but also a band, a drink, a drug, a dance club, a perfume, a café, a movie, a preschool, a pop song; a psychedelic music festival; Sexy Wonderland Erotic Cinema in Hamburg, Germany; and a special breed of Wonderland pansies bred by an elderly British guy called Gerald. There are other amusement parks, too—one in Canada, and another one near Beijing. Or rather, there used to be. It appears that the developer of the Beijing location went bankrupt and the park was abandoned before construction could be completed.

On my application form, I had explicitly indicated "acting" under special skills, underlined in pink felt tip pen. I am still waiting for them to find the right placement for me. All mascot roles are currently filled.

In the meantime, my laminated name tag reads *Happy Singh Soni, Wonderland Assistant*. Everyone who works here has the same name tag, though we'd all applied for different positions. At our first team meeting, I wasn't surprised to see Rajeev's eldest boy, Manni, and our former P.E. teacher. Satish now works at the ticket booth. We are a team of teenagers, primary school teachers, daily wagers, mechanics, plumbers, hawkers, musicians, dancers. None of us was hired for our old talents, so we had to adapt and transform, ripple and flow, acquiring new skills, hard and soft, fluid, seeping, and very mushy indeed, becoming better versions of ourselves. This is Wonderland after all.

Wonderland, Jalandhar: a truly global collage of nonstop fun. You might find minor resemblances to Disneyland rides, yes. A faint inkling of familiarity, too, in the curvy typo of the Wonderland logo. Like Disneyland, we've got a fair and lovely Snow White. Our squirrel mascots are proper Punjabi three-striped ones, though—not just knockoffs of Chip 'n' Dale, as you might assume. In the Ramayana there's this bit about a tiny squirrel trying to help the larger animals build a bridge—though they laughed at his efforts, Rama blessed the squirrel by stroking his back with three fingers. Hence the three stripes. Our Wonderland squirrels carry baskets of marigolds to distribute among the guests at the park entrance. In Punjabi, there's an expression that goes, *Kaato Fullaan Te Khed Di.*

Happy as a squirrel on flowers.

GENERATION HAPPY

I am the youngest of four; an afterthought, an accident. On the day I was born, I was welcomed by three siblings, all more than ten years my senior: Davinder, Fatehpal, and Ambika.

When my parents named me, they were obviously feeling fancy. All my siblings received proud, traditional names. Babbu, after reading a newspaper article on the future of farming in Punjab (basically, it was doomed), wished for me to find success internationally. Hence, on a whim, they chose a universal name, the most international name they knew: Happy. A name for a new generation in Punjab. People *had* to adore a boy called Happy. Right?

My parents assumed they were creating a popular kid. A sporty star of a boy. Field hockey hero, top of the class, genius in math and physics, which they valued highly. Instead, I grew up to be tall and lanky, with weird hair and a penchant for writing rambling, fantastical stories, brimming with unlikely characters, unable to distinguish the important from the unimportant. This, by the way, is a direct quote from a note one of my teachers had written next to a third-grade essay on "My Future Profession." His full remark reads as follows:

Happy Singh is an eager and lively pupil with an extensive vocabulary, but poor grammar, who, unfortunately, is unable to distinguish the important from the unimportant in his writing. His stories are brimming with unlikely characters who display values and habits foreign to our motherland. I seriously question whether he has a firm grasp of what is real and what is not.

I had a habit of humming popular Bollywood songs during math tests, which I failed, always. In my mind, I was dancing in front of crows, I mean crowds, but I had no talent for complicated choreographies in real life. I cut my hair with my mother's fabric scissors and wore it combed across my forehead in a floppy way, in an homage to Hugh Grant in *Notting Hill*. As this wasn't my hair's actual growth direction, it kept flopping back stubbornly. The haircut was the final straw for my parents, and my teachers, too. They declared me a lost cause. Which actually resulted in me getting just what I needed to hatch my dreams: peace and solitude.

Typical daydreams feature me formulating acceptance speeches for international film awards. My plan is to become an actor who plays the melancholy roles; the sad, pretty boys, rare in Indian cinema.

There are macho leads and funny boys en masse, but if you're looking for depth and vulnerability, you have to make up your own heroes. People (Ambika) tell me I'd be perfectly cast as the comedic side-kick, but that's no way to create a legacy.

So I practice a faraway look on my face, a gaze of pain and long-ing, like I'm really lusting for a third sugar roti at breakfast. If the acting thing doesn't work out, I'll turn to my second passion: screenwriting.

The double-lined notebooks from Mr. Tuli's Stationary Shop are my closest companions. I collect them underneath my bed in an empty sweets box, still emanating the milky-buttery scent of barfi, hidden behind rolled-up balls of sweaty sports socks, which are never used to play sports. When I finally do leave home, the box will con-tain up to nine plays, one half-written novel (and many hopeful beginnings), countless clumsy drawings, and a series of bad love poems that I never sent to the person I dedicated them to.

A LIST OF RESIDENTS OF SONI SQUARE—PUNJAB LAND RECORDS

BABBU SINGH AND GULWINDER KAUR SONI (PAPAJI AND MAMAJI): 1948–PRESENT

Babbu and Gul were assigned this land after Partition. Babbu purchased 100 rupees worth of cabbage seeds (of the Pride of India variety) and five water buffaloes, then took out a loan for a Mahindra & Mahindra tractor. And thus, Soni Farm was born.

HARMPREET SINGH BALLU (CABBAGE PICKER IN CHIEF): 1954–1994

A renowned cabbage expert, Harmpreet joined the farm as a picker when he was eighteen, and died from a stroke on the field during harvest, aged fifty-nine.

MANPREET KAUR BALLU (MRS. CABBAGE PICKER IN CHIEF): 1952–1995

Rekha look-alike and dhal connoisseur; mended my doll Leela when I ripped it trying to see what's inside. Now lives with her daughter Gurpreet's family in Kapurthala.

GURPREET KAUR BALLU (CABBAGE PICKER IN CHIEF'S DAUGHTER): 1972–1995

An excellent tractor driver, Gurpreet has three girls, one of them a nurse-in-training whom Gul consults via telephone for health advice.

RAJEEV SINGH BALLU (CABBAGE PICKER IN CHIEF'S SON & SUCCESSOR): 1977–PRESENT

Harmpreet's son, Rajeev, took over as Cabbage Picker in Chief and is working with us to this day.

BINNU, BALWINDER, MANNI (DAILY WAGERS): 1995–PRESENT

Balwinder showed me how to whistle, and the tech savvy Manni sometimes helps me film episodes for Happy TV. Binnu once saved my life.

RAJVINDER KAUR SONI: 1953

PARAMVEER KAUR SONI: 1955

AMRIT SINGH SONI: 1964

For each of my siblings gone before they were even born, Babbu planted a small fruit tree behind the house: amla, lemon, and mango. The amla tree died during the big drought of 1987, but the other two have grown tall by now; Gul makes an excellent green mango achar.

FATEHPAL SINGH SONI: 1970–1993

My eldest brother moved to Germany, where he has many different jobs. He got married to a German woman called Frida, which caused a bit of a scandal around here. They have two girls, my nieces Nastassja and Rani, whom I have never met.

DAVINDER SINGH SONI: 1974–2004

The light switch in the living room has been broken for almost a year. Since he has been gone, no one knows how to repair it.

AMBIKA KAUR SONI: 1978–2005

When I was fourteen, my sister got married and moved into a big house in Jalandhar. Her daughter, Amanjot, is eighteen months old.

HAPPY SINGH SONI: 1991–PRESENT

This is me. :)

A COLONY OF FIRE ANTS: 1948–PRESENT

Their foraging workers steal jaggery and besan from our kitchen. No one has found a way to keep them at bay.

SEVEN EMINENT WATER BUFFALOES: 1992–PRESENT

A HERD OF BEETAL GOATS (FLUCTUATING): 1950–PRESENT

Characterized by hanging ears and stubbornness. I am very fond of our goats, and abstain from eating goat stew, even if it smells delicious.

A SWARM OF DIAMONDBACK MOTHS (FLUCTUATING): 1999
The moths' pale green larvae love cabbage even more than I
love sugar rotis.

**A MURDER OF CROWS: SINCE THE BEGINNING OF TIMES AS WE
CHOSE TO COUNT IT.**

I STUCK OUT MY TONGUE
AND TASTED THE SKY

When I first arrived in his world, all I could see was shadow and light,
black and white; a line, a circle, an oval, and a square. My eyes got
tired quickly, but my mouth needed to be busy at all times; it was
made to drink sweet yellow milk. I searched for my mother's nipple
with my lips, my nose, and my fingertips. Even when there was just
air, I kept sucking it, like a giant honeybee would suckle nectar with
its straw-like mouth. I stuck out my tongue and tasted the sky—diesel
fumes and hot light.

I needed to touch, to suckle, to hold.

My body was wrapped in a shawl the color of rapeseed blossoms.
It was bound tight and calm. I kicked my legs against the fabric. It
loosened. I wiggled my toes.

Soon, my eyes learned how to stay open for longer periods of time.

I chased a ray of sun with my eyes.

I sneezed.

I could see legs: long legs, short legs, thin legs, chubby legs,
brown legs with black hairs, legs in loose brown cotton, legs clad in raw

silk, legs attached to bare feet with hairy toes in dusty blue flip-flops. Some legs I could cling to—they wouldn't shake me off. I could wrap my arms around them, hold them tight, breathe into their sun-warmed skin—they were mine. I squeezed their calves with my fingers and felt the hard tendrils of muscles until large hands came to loosen the grip of my small fists. I captured my father's big toe. It was an odd-looking object: bulbous and coarse. The nail was thick, yellowish, and hard. It fit my hand perfectly. I tried to pull it off. Lifting my head, I looked up into his face. Underneath his beard, Babbu smiled. I learned to recognize a smile. I saw there were different faces—round and longish, bearded and soft , generous and greedy, diffident and guarded—some mouths big and slurpy and others tiny and dry. I learned to recognize the legs and the feet, too: they belonged to people I loved. The second thing I ever felt in this world: after need came love.

My mother would set me down on the rug by the porch whenever she was preparing meals at the outdoor tandoor. Gul throwing a soft ball of dough from one hand to another, so fast it blurred, kneading it with her fists until she got tired, then rolling it out into perfect circles. A sizzling sound when she placed the shapes on the black tawa. Smoke rose, the shapes billowed and threw bubbles. The scent of rotis and ghee, which I archived in my Library of Good Smells.

The fire of the tandoor exuded a magnetic pull. I wanted to reach, to touch, to eat the dancing flames. Gul pulled me away from the fire, back onto the rug, again and again. Her hands were strong and covered in flour.

I stretched out my hands and found a smooth cool funnel made from stainless steel. It shone in the incandescent light of noon. I held it up to my face and saw a brown oval on its surface. The oval had eyes.

Davinder threw his crumpled field hockey clothes in a heap for Gul to wash by the well. I crawled inside his shirt and fell asleep. Sometimes, he brought fresh sugarcane when he came home from work. He kneeled down next to me, spliced it open with a shiny knife, and removed the hard green skin. I sucked on it the whole day, until the sweet juice was spent and the dry fibers got tangled in between my first front teeth.

I picked a piece of soft-boiled aloo from Ambika's plate. My greedy tongue whirled it right to the back of my throat. Everything stopped. I couldn't breathe. She thumped my back so hard I toppled over. I coughed the potato piece into her hand. I cried. She scolded me, but held me tight until I calmed down. Her hair smelled like cooking oil.

Fatehpal lay down on his back and put me up on his knees so I could spread my arms and fly on his legs as he swung them up and down. He was singing a song:

Fly up, Happy, Happy, fly up high, your mother loves you, your sister loves you, your father loves you, he works in the fields, the crows they fly, they will be here forever, and so will you, and so will you, and so will you.

THE COTTON CANDY KING

The Cotton Candy King of Jalandhar has been missing a thumb for as long as he can remember. When he was a kid, he snuck up to the roof and lit all the Diwali rockets he could find. The last one wouldn't light. And then he hadn't been quick enough to run away.

Well worth it. The sky of the village was illuminated for several minutes, thanks to me. It was like the end of a movie. When they carried me away from the roof, leaving a bloody train on the stairs, I smiled. Before I fell unconscious, that is.

You'd imagine the Cotton Candy King to be a plump and jolly man, but he is wiry, and has a face like a bullet, hard and closed off—unless you make him laugh, which I regard as my main task at Wonderland, taking it more seriously than my work as Security Liaisons Officer of the Rocky Ride. I can't tell King's age. He belongs to the realm of myths and exists outside real time—but he must be ancient. In spite of our age difference, we've been work buddies from day one. I'm used to doing things alone, so it feels good to be part of a team of two.

King is an exception to the rule for Wonderland personnel. We'd all had to undergo a three-day training so as to be adaptable to any park task, but his core skill proved too specialized to squander. King, he does the real thing, spinning actual fresh cotton candy, not like those hawkers selling them wrapped in plastic, propped up on a stick like big balloons. My stomach had lit up like a disco ball when I first saw that I'd been assigned to the Rocky Ride, where King's cart is permanently stationed. From my designated post, I can watch King as he crouches over his silver bowl, spinning the wheel until the sugar blurs and disappears, flying to the moon and back, cloud growing fine and mighty. Spinning sugar and air to spectacular effect is the work of a genius.

Watching King triggers one of my favorite memories: Davinder taking me along to see my first movie at the cinema hall in Jalandhar, when I was barely tall enough to reach the ticket counter.

He'd bought me a Limca with a red-and-white straw—and a huge cotton candy.

The movie Davinder chose had been an action flick called *Koyla*. I sank into my seat, letting the fire of the opening credits wash over me, following Shah Rukh Khan as he ran through a mountainous landscape with a pack of German shepherds, faster than lightning, to catch a black bird with his bare hands. While the plot is hazy, the memory of my first cotton candy is vividly imprinted on my tongue. When the lights came up, I was still clutching the syrup-smeared wooden stick tightly, reluctant to return to reality.

Now, whenever King hands me the stick with a cloud larger than my head, I beam as if I've been gifted the moon itself, believing in his artistry for all eternity.

I AM COTTON CANDY

I am a flitter, a puff up, and a flirt, merchant of sugary air, employed in the business of fat and furious dreaming. I am a universal temptation, timeless as such, a powerful people pleaser, known for charm and abundance. An apparition far bigger than the sum of my individual elements. Blown out of proportion, you see. Forgive me if I smile too wide, for it is a smile too wide that is expected of me.

Unable to dance, hop, twirl, or touch, possessing neither legs nor hips nor opposable thumbs—it does sadden me, true. Whenever it comes to mind. But my mind is a fickle thing. Neon lights or heavy winds will blow it apart, heavy rains dissolve it, easily. Liquid does what liquids do. I will melt on your tongue, saliva will reduce me to sugar, and then, nothing but juice and air. I will slip down your throat reluctantly—a hesitance to let go is natural to me, clingy as I am.

You, on the other hand, you should let go. Let go of the fear. Bite me, bite me, like there is no concept of tomorrow, and no such thing as common decency. No teeth? No problem. Lips will do. You cannot bite a cloud, you say? Then lick me. Lick me if you can. See if you can catch me, love, the wondrous essence of me.

Your lips and your tongue will take on my color; a souvenir.

I am a cloud spun out of sugar and air. You covet me and I adore you. I am cotton candy, and we are a match made in heaven. Once upon a time in the future, in a city beautiful, you will pass me by, and I will be waiting, perfectly spun, with a breath that is baited, ready to be placed upon your eloquent tongue.

THE DIAMONDBACK MOTH

Moths do not bleed, but crumble to dust. I'd squash their diaphanous wings like paper, porous from age or fire.

The diamondback moth infestation of 1999 almost left us bankrupt.

You see, it is neither the eggs nor the unremarkable moth, but the greedy larvae who cause toil and trouble for the cabbage farmer. Most likely of European origin, the diamondback moth is found throughout the Americas and in Southeast Asia, Australia, and New Zealand as well. Northern Punjab isn't their home; God knows how they found their way to our village. They might have been carried by the wind, just in time to feast on our juicy fledgling cabbage heads, before they could grow strong and mighty.

The eggs are scattered on the surface of foliage, translucent, appearing as green as the cabbage leaves; thus, they hatch in hiding, in just five days, most efficiently.

The larvae never sleep. Colorless at first, they grow into a soft electric green, radiating hunger. They move, push, shove, chew, and wriggle violently if disturbed by an animal or a pinkie finger, spinning down hysterically on a strand of silk. Requiring a large intake of fuel, they feed on the leaves between the thick veins and midribs, gnawing on the lower leaf's skin, leaving the upper epidermis intact. They will stunt the growth of cabbage heads, ultimately killing them off entirely.

Pupating in loose silk cocoons, the adult moth is slender and mud brown, unremarkable except for the cream diamonds along their back, and rather expressive antennae. The moths are weak fliers. However, they are readily carried by the wind.

I admired that quality. I, too, would like to be carried by the wind, readily. How clever they are, really, to be as efficient in their feasting as possible. Still, we had to kill them all. I not only squashed the moths, but collected the larvae, too, whenever I could spot them, tossing them into our chickens' greedy beaks like a prize. Later that night, I'd kept on catching them in my dreams, feeling phantom larvae wriggle in my fists, still clenched tightly. I believed I had single-handedly saved our farm that day.

But the next morning, my father found the chickens limp and dead. They looked green around the eyes, lying in contorted shapes, as if they'd died in agony, trying to escape a force that was already inside of them. I was guilty of their death.

Babbu asked a neighboring farmer for help, who brought over a canister marked with skull and bones, but the only thing the poison did was cause a red-hot rash on Babbu's hands and arms, turning brown skin pink after it healed.

We could save neither poultry nor cabbage in 1999. The larvae doubled, tripled, quadrupled, thriving, penetrating layer by layer, turning the cabbage leaves into a filigree of holes, until only dry corpses were left; memories of a glorious plump cabbage that once was.

HAPPY TV

On the way home from Wonderland, on the Rue du Bird, I am listening to "Masakali" from the movie *Delhi-6*. My amble turns into a dance. I mimic throwing a dove into the sky, opening my palms toward the horizon; then I fly right after her to meet the sun as it's about to set, burning, melting down into the ground, only to rise, throw, and burn once more. This is a good one; worth filming. I prop up my phone by a telegraph pole and start again, this time throwing myself flat on the ground at the end, to greater effect. No one is clapping. I jump up and bow twice nonetheless, making sure my smile reaches the fans sitting all the way in the back. I press Stop and try to upload the video on my channel, Happy TV, typing *Sunset Dance Number 1* into the Title field. But my mobile service is too slow. Maybe I need to charge my phone when I get home.

The crows are assembling in the gulmohar tree. It used to be that the tree was a marker of welcome, a sign that the visitor was now treading on Soni land. Now, it is simply a tree by a road, next to the tall walls of Wonderland. I am convinced the gulmohar tree doesn't like being the crows' meeting place at dusk and dawn. She is far too gentle for the birds' boisterous attitude. Blossoms in stages of decay from fiery red to rust and mud cover the path alongside the tree's pale trunk, curved and twined in a soft dance. I inhale the sweet smell of rot and pick up a particularly mushy flower to keep as an olfactory study.

I AM A GULMOHAR TREE

I am a gulmohar tree, and you know it; for it is June, and I am in full bloom.

I have been hatching in Punjab, Pakistan, and hence forward growing in Punjab, India, for over fifty years. I still call it my new earth, after all this time.

I am a gulmohar tree, but I must confess, I am unsure of my true identity.

All these blossoms, they are rather heavy, you see. They don't feel like "me." I let them rot and shake them off as soon as I can. Inflorescence of the brightest kind seems a little bit too much for my personality. When an introvert is gifted with such loud colors—well, I just don't know how to handle it most of the time.

For half a century I have been suffering from an illness that rarely befalls trees like me. It is called imposter syndrome. The term didn't even exist in my adolescence. Now I know it has a name, this odd itchy feeling.

When the attention once again becomes too much, I resort to humming a low tune, more a vibration than anything else; it calms me down.

Once I breathe to the rhythm of my own drum, I can overcome the fact that I am too large to hide. I am permanently exposed; in plain view.

My canopy can house creatures big and small, even clandestine rendezvous. My humming lulls to sleep the tiniest grasses and roadside flowers assembled around my trunk. In my dreams, I become a marigold; one of many, indistinguishable from one another.

The way people look at me has changed. For the longest time, they'd used their eyes; now, they hold up sleek small screens, filtering my light through a lens unseen. Whenever people photograph my flaming crown, I'd quite like to disappear.

I was most comfortable when I was still a seedling.

Snug, tuck, darkness, closely, pocket, silence. Prowess fast asleep.

The urge to grow was overpowering, and yet I resisted it for as long as I could. Gul nearly threw the pot away. She grew impatient for the sight of a green sprout in the black earth. In the end, the growth imperative is a force far bigger than you: you simply must shoot upwards, unless you'd like to implode and die from all that unused energy.

AISHWARYA RAI BACHCHAN

Our house is crammed next to the tall piss-yellow walls of Wonderland, like a letter in a long word on a too-short piece of paper. The rest of the farm was torn down to make way for the Thunder Dance and Wonderland Water World. Gul claims she's had to listen to the *Love Aaj Kal* soundtrack for days on end, and could I please ask Mr. CEO to change the tune, maybe a Madhuri Dixit flick?

The interior is gloomy. A perpetual dusk or dawn kind of light, pouring a soft brown tinge over fabrics, floor, and skin. It smells of rice and ghee. Sweet, powdery, and dry.

Gul is throning on her charpoy in the middle of the room, right where I left her this morning. The daybed is her usual spot, if she isn't at the kitchen going through the household expenses in her little book of numbers. The Red Fort's Peacock Throne would have been more fitting, but a daybed was what she got. She uses it with airs and affection. The remote control is an elongation of her limbs. Nobody else ever gets to use it. We must ask her to change the channel, knowing full well she might ignore it at will. Right now, she is watching *Koffee with Karan*. Aishwarya Rai Bachchan and Abhishek Bachchan are laughing on-screen, pearly teeth exposed, bright lights accentuating their glowing complexions. They are both smartly dressed in black. Aishwarya's eyes are a golden shade of green, supernaturally huge and light. For a second, her irises seem to be floating offscreen, hovering midair to meet me. Then they settle back in her eyes, and she closes them demurely.

GUL AND BABBU

I like to listen to the triad of Gul's creaking feet, the rustle of her chunni, and her sighs in the mornings. The sounds of her body and the gentle shushing of the gas stove are my wake-up calls. That and the smell of black tea leaves and cardamom, appeased by fatty milk. When I was younger, I had helped her peel the cardamom pods open and extracted the black seeds with my small fingers, putting a few in my mouth before I threw the rest into the boiling tea; sharp and sweet and much better than chewing gum.

She strains the tea, puts the kitchen in order, and updates her small book of numbers, scribbled minuscule in green ink, and then settles on her charpoy, positioned just so that it gives her a prime view of the TV. After a fast-paced news bulletin—Gul murmuring a prayer whenever a particularly gruesome piece of news is reported—renowned astrologer Anjali Sweety Parekh reveals the connection between celestial and terrestrial dynamics. This is my cue to leave for work, but my curiosity always gets the better of me, and I tend to hover behind Gul with my tea, enthralled by Anjali's prophecies and predictions. Will my second house enter Venus before sordid Taurus takes over and kills all lightness of being?

Before I leave, my mother usually presses a list into my hands of things to bring home from the local pharmacy. Gul has suffered from peculiar pains and imaginary ailments for as long as I can remember. She likes to visit doctors so they can tell her she is healthy and well:

Flourishing like a tree in bloom, Mrs. Soni. You will live to be a hundred and ten!

Gul makes them prescribe plenty of pharmaceutical products nonetheless, just in case. An array of brown paper bags from Jalandhar's preeminent pharmacies have accumulated in the kitchen cupboards: they contain natural herbs like neem and brahmi, as well as fat pink Nurofen, modest slim ibuprofen, and rust-red iron supplements. A special drawer contains the stronger stuff, for her back pain. These goodies make her soft and drowsy. Rare moments of tenderness unfold when she sucks on those small beige lozenges. She draws me into her dimply arms and ruffles my hair; afterward, she never remembers what she'd told me in those moments.

Growing up, whenever someone in the family fell ill, Gul flourished. She came to life, eyes glistening and mind racing, listing the herbs, tinctures, and food with healing properties that she needed to prepare. We weren't to see a doctor; she simply prescribed an assortment of remedies from her own personal pharmacy. Lying in bed with a stomach flu when I was about five, I remember how she walked through the room, singing prayers, burning incense and bell peppers.

The only one to refuse her treatments is Babbu. When he catches a cold, he rolls himself up into a wooly scarf cocoon, sipping tea poured from a white thermos beside his bed. He refuses to talk, claiming it hurts his head, and rewatches the field hockey world cup of 1994. Babbu was a childhood nickname that stuck with him. No one can recall his real name. He is Babbu, that's it. Babbu Singh Soni moves and speaks at the speed of his thinking, which is unhurried and meticulous. His ideas are based on careful observation of the world, done through gentle, mole-like eyes behind thick horn rims. He has a big stubby nose and a well-tended gray beard. He prefers the company of crows to that of people. Every morning he goes out to feed the birds with stale roti crumbs; his "me time." He wears a dark red turban, except for the days when he used to wash his hair in the courtyard with my brothers and me, back when we were still complete. I would watch the fragrant, foamy trickle of water disappear into the dirt behind the ice-cold well, pretending it was a stormy sea for my toy boats. I imagined them going down the drain and disappearing forever. I have always been fascinated by disappearing acts: things simply dissolving, like a fizzy aspirin in a glass of water, or my head in Gul's arms.

SUGAR ROTIS

Starving, I shuffle around for leftovers, sending a stack of freshly scrubbed stainless steel plates tumbling. Without lifting her eyes from the screen, Gul shushes me and impatiently gestures toward the stove, her forehead arranged in countless tender folds, face illuminated by the rapidly changing lights of the TV. Aloo parathas and sugar rotis are waiting for me, neatly wrapped in aluminum foil. She'd left her throne to prepare them, so they would be ready by the time I got home.

I start with the sugar rotis, tearing the foil open without even sitting down. The inside is warm and moist. Fresh off the tawa.

Crispy moon landscape wrapped around sweet juice. Burnt craters, floury planes, sugary lowlands, and those secret places where the filling has leaked, touching the pan, caramelizing, burning. Syrup is bound to drizzle down the sides of your mouth and run down your fingers when you eat sugar rotis. And that's exactly how it should be. Roll them up and dip them in cold creamy buffalo yogurt for utter perfection.

Close the fridge, Happy! What a waste of energy.

Later, spread-eagled across my charpoy, I can't fall asleep. It's too hot, I am too full. I wish we had AC. I wish I was in Switzerland. I listen to the hum of the old ventilator, blue paint splintering off, drowning out the chatter and clapping of the late-night talk shows— Gul keeps the TV on all night, relying on the sound to sleep soundly, while Babbu retires in a separate room with a blanket up to his nose and toilet paper stuffed down his ears. I pick up my phone and check my YouTube channel. "My Sunset Dance" has ten views. I rewatch it. I should have optimized the sound quality. I need to professionalize. Technical equipment is needed urgently. But as it is, the Europe funds are a priority. I collect my earnings in an empty barfi box underneath my bed. After swiping through the latest in our Wonderland group chat (*don't leave discarded sweet wrappers at the workplace; remind customers to take their sunglasses off for the rides!!!; don't slouch; smile; hide beneath your booth when you take a sip of water*) I open my browser to conduct my nightly research.

Flights to Switzerland: too expensive to even dream about. Flights to Germany: not entirely out of the question, though it would take several years of saving my entire income. Flights to Italy: realistic, as early as next spring, were I to take a one-way flight to Rome. I google travel agents near me: Manni Singh, Tagra Travel, Karamveer Singh's Travel Agency. Karamveer looks jolly in the picture on his website. I note down their numbers. I drift off to sleep while adding up rupees in my head, never quite reaching a satisfactory sum.

GUL: IBU 800

1. rapeseed honey and cough syrup

2. Ibu 800

3. new tawa (Jalandhar market—Ambika?)

4. ask Rajeev's son to help pack up kitchen utensils

5. how to record things on TV?—who can help?!

6. kitchen tap repair—who to ask?! cost? (Ambika)

7. mend Happy's work trousers, get purple thread

Hip pain today—OK. Only when I bow down to pick up the stuff Happy scatters around the floor. He's late today. Sugar rotis waiting.

THEY CARRIED LITTLE

Babbu and Gul disappeared from their old life at the time of the Partition, when they left Punjab in what is now Pakistan for Punjab in India. The knowledge I have about the Partition has been carefully assembled over years.

Babbu had intended to travel alone across the newly formed border, to make sure they had a home in Jalandhar, that everything was safe and sound before his young wife's arrival. But Gul was convinced that if she let him depart on his own, they would never see each other again. She insisted on coming with him straight-away. Only seventeen at the time, she already had a will of iron. They carried little. They were sure they would return. Unable to take a direct route because of the riots, they were forced to make a detour to the border in Jammu and Kashmir. I tried to trace their escape route on the map once. It looked like an odd wilting flower. Circles, slanted lines, undulating waves; the ambiguous paths of a splitting in two.

Babbu and Gul rarely talk about it. There was no room to dwell, in between cabbage and children and dealing with unforeseen farming challenges such as the Drought of 1987. Still, I did my research. I was curious; I've never liked a puzzle with missing pieces. Whenever I asked too many questions, Gul's eyes started looking for the remote control.

They've been residents of Soni Square for more than fifty years, but still, deep down, they are people on the move. They've never returned to their old village. Over time, they forgot its buildings, its people, its cattle, its flowers, and its particularly rich buffalo milk, foamy and warm in a jug made of clay. The place of their birth has taken on a strange and shifting shape; an image drawn in sand, sieved through multiple eyes and ears, losing contour. By now, they've almost forgotten its name.

I AM A NECKLACE THAT IS SPLIT

I am a necklace that is split. I am not one, but many. Six jade beads of the lightest green, three pendants of agate-jasper. Between them are wooden beads shaped like plates, separating and connecting all at once. Another six of my beads are missing; I know they are in Delhi, but I am not sure of the exact location. I can still feel them, though, like phantom limbs. When human hands touch me, they only do so in white gloves.

I was made before the beginning of time as you know it. The place of my birth has been named Mohenjo-daro, when the big naming of things happened. The naming and assigning and the structuring; the classifying, the rectifying, and the writing down in books; archiving, owning, loaning, and bemoaning.

I remember my first neck: it was brown like yours. I haven't felt skin in over fifty years, and yet I am made to be felt: to rub and knead and massage and stroke. To touch and be touched. To become more and more of a pearl, a pore, breathing, contracting, and expanding; a smoothling and a roundling thing. A thin layer of fibers separates me from any real contact at all. I am surrounded by a membrane of dreams long lost.

Could you hold me once? When no one is looking, with the tip of your pinky finger. The risk, really, is minuscule. I can promise you that.

I would like to touch rather than speak. Words are insufficient, always. I have lived so many lives, and grand parts of it have been spent in silence.

They split me at the time when they drew the line across the country. They drew a line across my beads as well and divided me in two. The result was two new necklaces altogether: my dearly departed in India and me. It hurt at first. The unthreading and threading and becoming anew, questioning your sense of self altogether—but over time I became comfortably numb. You can get used to anything, really. Anything at all.

I am glad they got me out of the fabric in my wooden drawer. I rarely see the light of day. The fabric makes it hard to breathe.

I must confess, because you gave me an inch, I will now ask for a mile. I know I only asked you to hold me once. And it did feel good, really. But more than anything, I would like to be made whole again. Could you assist me in my quest? Simply take me out of my pouch, put me in your pocket; I can see that it is large and roomy, I will be most comfortable there. The journey from Lahore to Delhi isn't a long one, you can book a ticket for tomorrow, bright and early. I have learned about the new modes of transport—aren't they a marvel? To think we can just fly. We are lucky, aren't we?

VOICEMAIL FROM GUL

Happy, you are not picking up. Why have you always got that little phone with you if you never pick up? You always told me, "I need a phone, I need a phone, what if there was an emergency?"

Thank God your sister picks up when I call, only one in the family who does. Just as I was starting a morning rerun of *Koffee with Karan*, someone called on the landline from that Wonderlandy company of yours, urgent question regarding when we'd be vacating the house, and Babbu wasn't around of course, sitting under the ber tree, as he does every morning, doing God knows what. You know how I hate wandering around the grounds, but they said to call back as soon as we could, so I hurried to get him and slipped on the stupid gravel. Can you believe I fell and couldn't get up by myself? Lying there, no one around but the sleeping dogs. My hip hurting badly, very badly! Finally, Manni found me, God bless. What would have happened to me otherwise?

He called Ambika, who arrived fast, you know her husband's car. We went to the doctor, the good one, nothing fractured. He prescribed some strong stuff for the pain. Very sleepy now . . .

The night before we left, I'd gone to get a bag of hot gobi pakoras while Babbu arranged for our next means of transport—gobi pakoras were his favorite back then, though, mind you, he never touched them again after that—not far till Jalandhar now. We were hopeful. On the way back to the hostel, I realized I was being followed by a group of men. It was dusk, I was seventeen, thin as a stick. God knows why they picked me. There were five of them. Heckling and cackling, maybe drunk on sugarcane liquor, calling me all kinds of names . . . I don't want to repeat them to your ears. I walked fast, you have never seen me rush along like that, taking public, crowded lanes, although, in those days, that wouldn't have made a difference. They caught up, started touching my arm, pulling at my dupatta. It was new, bright blue with golden seams, already ruined from the dust of the road. I felt dirty, we hadn't washed properly in a week. I kept my eyes on the ground, didn't want to encourage them, you see. When I looked up briefly, I saw a red cross on white ground, a sign for a hospital. God bless my good eyes. They are still excellent, no glasses needed. A matter of willpower.

When I saw the cross, I ran as fast as I could. The foyer of the hospital smelled of iodine and old people. Now I am old myself, of course . . . It was filled with people, the nurses couldn't manage the intake. I stayed for the whole night, huddled in a corner by the reception, not daring to look at anyone. My toes were curled the entire time. I only noticed after, when day broke and I finally unclenched my feet. I needed some time till I could get up, my limbs had fallen asleep. Sure, they found another girl that night. The migraines started then, went on for months, even after we had arrived. They still return, you know, from time to time . . .

Babbu meanwhile, waiting back in the overcrowded hostel, pacing a hallway full of outstretched limbs and bundles with essential belongings—he was sure I'd died. He'd been scared to leave the guest house and go looking for me, in case he missed my return. But later, he beat himself up over the fact that he hadn't accompanied me that night. No portable phones back then, in case of emergency, no nothing. We had to hope and pray, that was all we had . . .

Anyway, I will see you when you get home. You always dawdle, doing God knows what on the way. Just don't expect your sugar rotis today, I can hardly move. New episode tonight. Can't stand the guy, but here we are. I started it, and now I have to watch every episode, or I feel I'm missing out.

VILLAGE TV

We got our TV in 1994. The first in the village. Babbu and Davinder brought the box home from Model Town market in Jalandhar, so big I could use it as a house for me and Leela, Ambika's ragged Rajasthani doll. By the time I got her, Leela's eyes had fallen off and her sari had faded from bright red into a shade of grayish pink. Because she was blind, I had to describe everything to her, giving a running commentary of the world as I saw it.

Gul was skeptical: *Where shall we put this thing? I don't under-stand the fuss. So expensive! And much nicer to watch on a big screen in a movie theater, no?*

The first thing I remember watching on TV, lying on my belly in front of the screen with Leela under my arm, was an ad for Dhara vegetable oil. A runaway boy, about my age, was being coaxed back home by the thought of his mother's jalebis, just as warm and golden as the jingle. Soon, I could hum it by heart—and I did, all the time, to my family's annoyance. Gul never made jalebis. She just needed to buy Dhara oil! I wanted to crawl inside the screen and live inside that ad.

Every memory I have is linked to the stuff I watched and the snacks I ate while watching. I sort the timeline of my life according to memorable film and food pairings. (I imagine this timeline like a large cartoonesque arrow, drawn in rani pink, softly vibrating through vast dark space.) Meanwhile, it is essential to match pro-grams with adequate watching partners, too. These pairings could look a little bit like this: watching the field hockey World Cup with Babbu while dipping Gul's crispy cabbage pakoras in cold raita; *Boogie Woogie Dance Show* with Ambika and mouthfuls of sweet makhani; Bruce Lee with Davinder and a bag of Punjabi tadka namkeen on my lap.

For the World Cup, Babbu set up the TV outside (Davinder had brought home a cable roll from work) so our neighbors could come and watch with us. Pakistan won, defeating the Netherlands 4–3. Babbu recorded it all. He kept rewatching the hockey game, ana-lyzing it, debating it with friends. We got a secondhand video recorder from Avtaar, a cousin twice removed, who was a well-known "organizer" of stuff: he opened up a whole new world of possibilities for us.

I was allowed to rest my head on Ambika's lap while she watched her *Boogie Woogie Dance Show*. I could feel her belly rising and falling with her laughs and hear Gul cluttering with her armada of containers in the kitchen—always, it was only a matter of time until she would call Bika to come and help. In my mother's view, an idle girl was the worst thing there was in the world.

Davinder was away quite often back then. He was working with the old electrician in town, saving money to start his own business. When he was at home, and wasn't out helping Babbu and the workers on the fields, he liked to relax and unwind with his VHS collection of Bruce Lee movies. He was Bruce's biggest fan—probably in the whole of India.

For TV and me, it was love at first sight. For Gul, her infatuation was more of a slow burn.

When I get home from work, I can already hear Karan Johar's voice at the front door.

The charpoy squeaks when I sit down next to her, sinking deep into the shape her body has prepared for me. The blue light illuminates both our faces as we watch silently, until I fall asleep, head tilting against her warm shoulder, to the pearlescent sound of a laugh track, and the smell of the menthol salve Gul uses to ease her back pains.

THE LOO INTERVIEWS

I unwrap the foil from yesterday's aloo paratha and take it outside, leaving my mother to watch tonight's program in peace. I pass the outdoor toilet, a slim stone hut built the same year of the Diamond Moth Infestation. Before then, the bathroom had been a spot behind the well where no grass grew. A hole, some straw, a water hose. When I first learned to use a toilet, squatting above a hole in the ground in the right position and at the right angle, I tried to get my parents or siblings to keep me company. Have a little chat, to aid the flow of energies. But they resisted, calling me a little stinker who couldn't keep his mouth shut. Of course, it wasn't the nicest place to be, smell-wise, atmospherically.

Whenever I needed a poo, I became a famous celebrity surrounded by paparazzi trying to click a picture. A beautiful exchange of energy: I poo, you get an exclusive with me, myself, and I. There I'd be, squatting in the outdoor toilet, disclosing personal information, getting things off my chest. The journalists of *Jodhpur News*, known for their merciless celebrity gossip, had neither boundaries nor inhibitions. For some reason they'd heard of me all the way in far-off Rajasthan. Three years old and already the beloved subject of a premiere print journalism series known as *The Loo Interviews*.

JODHPUR NEWS: Hi, Happy Singh. How are you today?
HAPPY: Fine, thank you. I can poop on my own. All alone!
JODHPUR NEWS: Marvelous. A great achievement. A big step
toward independence. Congratulations!

HAPPY: Thank you. [beaming]

JODHPUR NEWS: I hear they call you the Prince of Cabbage Land.

HAPPY: I like cabbages. I like to see them get big. Some get huge! Look, like this!

JODHPUR NEWS: Oh, watch your feet, don't fall, son! Keep your hands on your knees for balance. What did you have for dinner, Happy Singh?

HAPPY: Rotis and spinach.

JODHPUR NEWS: What else did you do?

HAPPY: I built a watering tank for the crows. So they can drink. No rain for a long time.

JODHPUR NEWS: I see. Are things going well at the farm?

HAPPY: Hmm, not so very well, I think. It is dry. And my father is scared of moths, you see.

JODHPUR NEWS: Do moths eat cabbage?

HAPPY: Yes. They have sharp gnarly teeth. I can't spot any teeth when I catch them, though. Maybe they are invisible!

JODHPUR NEWS: Are they big, those moths? Do they eat little boys, too?

HAPPY: Nooo. No, they couldn't eat me. Their mouths are tiny. Tiny mouths with gnarly teeth.

JODHPUR NEWS: Good to know. So, you are safe. Are you scared you will fall into the hole?

HAPPY: I make sure that I won't fall. My brothers taught me how to squat the proper way. Otherwise, I wonder . . . Would I fall through the earth? Down, down, down . . . What would be on the other side?

JODHPUR NEWS: I'd have to look it up—but you might find yourself somewhere in the ocean off the coast of Chile.

HAPPY: Chili?

JODHPUR NEWS: Chile—a slim and rather extraordinary country in South America. Well, you won't know until you try.

HAPPY: But I don't dare try. My parents would miss me very much, I should think.

JODHPUR NEWS: Well, OK. Whatever you think is best, Happy Singh.

HAPPY: I am finished now.

JODHPUR NEWS: Marvelous.

HAPPY: I think I will go back inside.

JODHPUR NEWS: Well, OK. Take care of yourself. Until next time.

The reporter closed his notebook and adjusted his small gold-rimmed glasses. He had been scribbling down my answers during our conversation but seemed slightly disappointed. I couldn't shake the feeling that he'd wanted something bad to happen, just so he had more of a story. I gathered the brightest stars on my way back to the bedroom, calling each by its name, Blinky, Pinky, Inky, and Clyde, and, when I fell asleep, I dreamed I was floating in a sea of chilies.

WONDERLAND GROUP CHAT:
VENDING MACHINE

HAPPY: @Manager D, I was wondering when the vending machine in the employee lounge will be restocked to full effect?

MANAGER D: plz refrain from asking again @Happy, will let u know once it arrives.

MR. CEO: urgent reminder @wlteam that there is no eating allowed on the job. only in designated areas.

SNOW

While I was busy writing a nine-page screenplay entitled *The Sad Dancer*, Kiran was shoveling buffalo shit. At least that's what he claimed. Kiran and I grew up together, but he left school early to help support his family. As a daily wager, he initially worked as a farm hand, and then moved on to Punjabi Paints, mixing huge pools of durable outdoor paint, the odors of which made him drowsy. He had been smoking since he was ten and soon transitioned to weed. Śānta hō jā'ō—*relax, mate*. This was his motto. He was happy to be a worker instead of a schoolboy. A real man. He boasted about the duress of his physical labor and pushed out his meager chest, which slowly became stronger because of all that heavy lifting.

Kiran smelled of sweat, cannabis, and poisonous solvents. I carried paper and ink on my skin, the scent of sweet ghee permanently entangled in my unkempt hair. Relative to him, I was tender, protected, spoiled. Kiran was everything I was not. For that, I adored him. I cast him as the sexy love interest in all my dreams. I would have died on the spot if he ever found out. Or rather, he might have taken the matter into his own hands. You see, Kiran and I, we weren't exactly what you might call friends. You might even say that he and his gang were bullying me quite severely.

Kuthi! he'd spit at me and laugh. *Can you see the fairy dust in his hair?*

Kiran's eyes were red and small.

I mostly hid or ran whenever I saw him. But I still heard all the rumors; mothers whispering to each other; whispering to their sons; fathers averting their eyes, nodding knowingly. *Snow.* I heard the word many times.

What could be evil about snow? I thought.

Then I saw for myself.

One day, I spotted him behind Punjabi Paints, crouched behind a heap of empty cartons. Kiran didn't even notice me passing. He didn't seem to notice anything around him. He closed his eyes and leaned back; lips contorted into a rapt half-smile. It was the smile of a snake in an old comic I used to read. The look on her face when she had spotted her prey. I tried to write down what I saw. Notebook in hand, pen poised, I couldn't quite grasp it nor bring it to paper. Instead, I drew a snake with a syringe. It looked like a bad tattoo.

Kiran continued working for a while; he needed the money. But his employers complained about his weak arms, his laziness, and never hired him again. He moved away, setting up camp outside the farms that employed him for a few days at a time; in the end he washed up in Kapurthala. He died shortly after he turned seventeen. On his sleeping mat by a field of blooming rapeseed, in the early hours, when things seemed a little more fragile than in the light of day. Gul told me about his death over breakfast one morning. It was the only day I'd ever not eaten a sugar roti. I left the table without eating anything at all.

I never understood the term "sexual orientation," which I'd read for the first time online in *Teen Vogue*. Why not "love directions"? For me, before the thought of sex had even surfaced, there was love. Nothing compares to the feeling of being enamored and discontent at age thirteen. Discontent because your love interest doesn't even know your name—or, worse, detests you up to the point of chasing you through a street throwing empty Limca bottles. But still, you feel as alive as you will ever be. It drives you to do all sorts of crazy things. For instance, it will make you write the worst love poems in the world, poems that no one will ever read.

K
I
R
A
N

Kiran,
I ran from you

But just know I'd watch you snooze
and get drunk without a drop of booze

Eyes like a muddy pond at noon
with tender algae
enlightened by a ray of sun.

Dreams:
sit behind you on a scooter
get lost in your curls
feed you barfi with my bare hands

Kiran,
you are the hero of the movie
I'll write in your honor
I'll be your organ donor

When it comes to the final scene
On the Paris motorway
Under a bodhi tree
I'll run to you and wrap your wounds
in white cloth
And dance for you to help you heal.

AMBIKA

When Ambika heard that Satish spilled his milk on me accidentally on purpose, she'd drenched his head in Limca. No hesitation, no questions asked. That was the kind of girl she was. Ambika always had a streak of wildness in her. You wouldn't know this by looking at her life right now, which is neat and tidy on paper. Heavily veiled under the right kind of clothes and her current world fabric, made up of home and husband and baby. But the certain something is still there: you never know what she's truly thinking. She is eloquent, a fast talker, a speedy thinker. She can talk to you and still be very much in her own world, thinking thoughts unknown, crossing boundaries in her mind. A freedom she finds inside of her, no matter what. It distances her from people. Some find her arrogant, some see a darkness in her, which makes her even more attractive to those of us who know better. There is hardly anyone in the world I respect and fear more than Ambika.

I couldn't comprehend why she got married so quickly. Her grades were the best in school, she would have gotten into college, a scholarship even. Whenever I ask her, she becomes irritable: *I made a decision. That's that.* I'd asked whether she'd been pregnant, and they'd had to tie the knot. A flat firm palm landed on my cheek, smelling of roses and onions at the same time, smacking with ease and vigor. Her slap left an angry red mark that stayed all day. After that, I didn't dare to ask anymore.

THE ACCIDENTAL LIBRARY

The library doesn't hierarchize, nor does it discriminate. It contains, amongst others, *Five on a Treasure Island*, a DVD of *Devdas*, Franz Kafka's *Amerika*, short stories by Saadat Hasan Manto, and Bertolt Brecht's *Mother Courage and Her Children* in the original German. The titles mostly belong to Mr. Tuli's own archive, collected over years in his shop; some are found, others are donated by people getting rid of books and other stuff. In our village, this happens only once in a decade, which explains the very real limitations of the accidental library. Yet I keep checking back every week, on the hunt for treasures unseen. Mr. Tuli and the accidental library are my own private university.

On a fateful day in 2004, the box did indeed contain something new: a collector's edition box set of movies by some guy called Godard, so thick I had to hold it with two hands.

I looked down at the portrait on the cover, of a dark-haired man, face painted bright blue, and a full-lipped woman with a stylish fringe, smoking lasciviously.

THE ABDUCTION OF EUROPA

A woman in a white sari is riding on a water buffalo. There is a cream rope attached to its neck—the woman is holding it quite elegantly, with her slim-fingered hand. Funny. You would actually need a bit more power to command a water buffalo.

She is seated sidesaddle, like a woman on the backseat of a scooter. I think she forgot to put her top underneath the sari. I can see her bare shoulders. Probably had to leave in a hurry.

The longer I look at the woman's face—she looks vaguely familiar. Where have I seen her before?

I put my hand over her body.

I imagine a turban on her head.

Maybe it's the shadow around her jaw.

Yes. She looks like a boy. An Indian boy. She looks a little bit like Kiran.

BANDE À PART

Three faces, eleven letters, underscored by tinkling piano notes:

B A N D E   À   P A R T E. The opening credits are superimposed onto a scene of traffic in the suburbs of Paris. A Citroën 2CV and a truck carrying Pernod pastis, a harbor and a large crane. The fog is here to stay. The sky, for the duration of the movie, remains slate gray. The title music is melancholy, elegiac.

We, the audience, are seated behind two men in a convertible. I can smell the seats: smoke and damp and leather. The driver's eyes flash in the rearview mirror: dark and handsome. He is whistling a song. The men are called Arthur and Franz. Franz (like Kafka?), who is telling the tale, is wearing a black fedora, accentuating his cheekbones. Arthur is wearing a less flattering cap on a world-weary face. Even before we encounter them, Franz and Arthur have been plotting a heist; a robbery. They are both, in varied shades, crooks: petty crooks, pretty crooks, silly crooks, crooks in pretend-love.

The female lead is Odile, une jeune fille romantique, riding a bike in a checkered pleated skirt. What makes her romantic? Is she romantic because she falls in love? Or because she thinks she needs people to fall in love with her?

In any case, she tries to decide whom she likes better: Arthur or Franz. But I think this is only because there is no one else around. Like how you fall in love with people at your school, or work place, just because they're *there*.

At Madison Café, the three have Coca-Cola, schnapps, and peppermint soda. They plan a robbery, dance a dance, and hold a minute of silence. Weird they don't eat anything throughout the entire movie.

THE LOO INTERVIEWS II

Some of the reporters at *Jodhpur News* swore I was beginning to resemble Sami Frey, a favorite of Godard's who plays Franz in *Band à part*. Others likened me to a young Franz Kafka, only not as pale, and with the ability to smile, demonstrating a bit more joie de vivre.

It seemed there had been a change in the editorial team. They were young, upbeat, and cosmopolitan. I noticed that their references had become a lot more refined.

JODHPUR NEWS: Happy Singh Soni. Lovely to meet you here in the great outdoors. Are you enjoying your poo en plein air?

HAPPY: I do enjoy myself, sir. I always do.

JODHPUR NEWS: Has anyone ever told you that you look like Sami Frey?

HAPPY: Thank you, sir. Very kind. I am, incidentally, a big fan.

JODHPUR NEWS: Oh, very well. Are you a fan of European cinema?

HAPPY: Absolutely. In particular, I have been educating myself in French cinema. When the mobile reception is decent, that is.

JODHPUR NEWS: Marvelous. Admirable, really. To gather all this knowledge, all by yourself. [Happy smiles, humbly.]

JODHPUR NEWS: So you do know he was a favorite of Godard's—

HAPPY: Yes, of course. My favorite movie is *Bande à part*.

JODHPUR NEWS: Why is that?

HAPPY: Well . . . I like the dance. I like the things Franz and
Odile say in the car. I like the ending. And the Indian Bird
of Death Franz talks about . . . although I never heard of
such a bird here in Punjab before.

JODHPUR NEWS: Splendid. I might investigate a little, see
whether I can find out more about that mysterious Bird of
Death. We have access to all kinds of archives and
resources. In any case, we are rooting for you, Mr. Happy!
We at *Jodhpur News* are all huge fans. Would you do me a
favor and sign these autograph cards for us?

I signed the cards, happily. The portrait looked like it had been
taken when I was asleep, with bits of spit accumulating at the corner
of my mouth. An odd choice, but an autograph card is an autograph card.

HAPPY TV: WHAT
I WANT TO BE
WHEN I GROW UP—
THE VILLAGE EDITION

"Ready? Camera rolling. Let's get started, shall we? OK then, first question—you know this is a series about the different professions in our village, yes?—so my first question would be, did you always know you wanted to be a Cabbage Picker in Chief?"

"My grandfather was a cabbage farmer. He lost the farm after Partition. My father was a cabbage picker, all his life, dropped dead on the field even—after the harvest was done. That's the kind of man he was. Dutiful till last breath. So now I'm a cabbage picker, too."

"OK. Great. Runs in the family, then. When did you start out in your profession?"

"Start out?"

"Like, at what age?"

"I think I was . . . eight years old. I was this tall." [Indicating a line across his belly.]

"That's very young."

"Not so very young, no."

"How did you find starting to work at such a young age?"

"Eight years is not young. I was strong. Tall for my age."

"You are still the tallest."

"Yes."

"Yes."

"You started helping with the goats, too, when you were a scrawny small thing. Ha. I remember, when they all ran loose, disappearing into the rapeseed field, one of them nearly killed by a tractor . . . your father came to the rescue, and I ran to catch the missing one. You cried like a baby."

"No need to sound so gleeful. Never happened again, did it? Always kept them all together, no matter how strenuous . . . actually, we might cut this bit . . . Now, the most important skill for a cabbage picker, what do you say?"

"Most important skill . . . that would be . . . First, know how to use a knife. How to sharpen it, maintain it, honor it. Know the earth. Know the cabbage. Beware of the snakes. Strong, you need to be strong, too. Moving, moving, all day long. No time for reading, idle flimsy nonsense and stuff . . ."

"Reading isn't being idle. It's brain work. It burns calories, you know."

"Yes, Happyji."

"Why are you chuckling like that?"

"Sorry, Mr. Big Shot. I'm just a happy person, that's why."

"OK. Where were we . . . right. So, any advice for future cabbage pickers?"

"Yes: Don't become a cabbage picker. Learn a proper profession. A profession that allows you to sit on your bottom all day, be idle, live longer. Also, I would like to greet my cousin in Kapurthala, and my little brother, the lucky idiot, if he ever made it to Europe and sees this: Send over some of your earnings, if you please. Second nephew on the way. Thank you. God bless."

"Ok then. I suppose . . . that's a wrap on the first interview in our new series, *What I Want to Be When I Grow Up—The Village Edition*. Thank you to Rajeev, our esteemed Cabbage Picker in Chief, and thank you to Manni, our cameraman. You can press stop now . . . No, you . . . Yeah, just here. Why are you still laughing? It would help if you'd take this a bit more seriously. You know, this is a real job, too. Almost. Could be one day."

NORTH AND SOUTH

The rapeseed plants are teenagers; proud, precocious, and tall. They accommodate me well while I watch clips of *Band à part* on my phone. I rewatch the movie many times, mostly at dusk. Looming over me are the telegraph poles and thick balls of intertwined cables leading all the way to Jalandhar and beyond, connecting me with future selves.

"I can't decide between the North and the South. You decide."

It's this one sentence, uttered by Franz in the car at the end of the movie, that I remember most vividly. It can be applied to numerous occasions in the life of an indecisive: At key moments in any story, there is always the decision between North and South. A decision between Ice or Fire, Light or Dark, Sweet Barfi or Bitter Gourds. I note it down and decide I will use it one day, if I ever do finish writing a screenplay.

CAREER DREAMZ PVT. LTD.

YOUR Dreams are OUR Reality
Arranging for your education abroad
Coordinating YOUR career dreams for YOU
Call NOW and live YOUR tomorrow TODAY
Free Career Consultation—Walk-Ins Welcome

WONDERLAND GROUP
CHAT: ALARM

MANAGER D: @HAPPY alarm @WL

MANAGER D: u need to go check and see what's the situation . . .

HAPPY: right now? almost 11 p.m. . . .

MANAGER D: u r the closest

HAPPY: what abt sajeev–security man?

MANAGER D: can't reach him.

HAPPY: OK, OK, I'll go and check . . . let me just get dressed

YOUR OFFICIAL INVITATION
TO EUROPE

The great hum in the sky has always been there. It is my constant companion. A steady background murmur, a vibration, the sum of all sounds of the universe—mostly taking on the form of a recent Bollywood tune. It gives me the buzz I need to dance in my mind. I need the hum. Possibly the hum needs me, too.

On my way home from Wonderland, I am humming "Breathe" by Pink Floyd. Then, a voice begins weaving in and out of the melody.

It sounds faraway, female, melodious—decidedly foreign. She is greeting me, I think.

But also, it kinda just sounds like she is practicing her lines.

Hello!
Hi.
Hiya!
Well, hullo there!
Sat Sri Akaal.
Are you there?
Hi there.
Lovely to meet you!
Over the moon to finally meet you, Happy Singh Soni—literally, just slid over the moon to meet ya. Lovely at this time of the year isn't it? If a little dark on the other side. You can see the bulbous, fiery form of Mars rising beyond the Tsiolkovsky crater. That brings me to

my credo: *Always look on the bright side!* But I know this is your motto, too.

I come from the Great Hum in the Sky, bearing good news: your official invitation to Europe, it has finally arrived. Look, here. Breathe in the air of freedom!

I know what you're thinking, Happy.

All that you cook, all that you stew, and all that you steam, all that you fry, all that you know, and all that you need, all that you smell, all that you feel, and all that you burn, all that you hope, all that you make, everything you ever ate. All that you draft, all that you write, all that you lie, all that you love, and all that you fear, all that you feel, and everything you think is real. All that you are, really.

I know you, Happy Singh Soni. I know you, and everything under the moon.

Full disclosure, this was my first gig as a representative of Europe. How did I do? You can rate my performance after this call. Full stars would be very welcome. Currently, I am just an assistant, with a promise of promotion, though—good things will happen soon. You are my first project. I really wanted to work with you, you see. I chose you and no one else.

Come to Europe!

Come as you are, ladidadida. Ha ha. Sorry. I'm being told I shouldn't laugh at the end of every other sentence. It's a sign of insecurity, really. Weakening the message.

OK then, I can see you are still processing. I will leave you to it. This is the official invite. Don't lose it. My contact details are to be found down there, below the small print. Europe is fine, no need for *last names. Don't forget to rate me, though. Ha ha. Sorry. Did it again. Oh dear.*

THE INDIAN BIRD OF DEATH

> FRANZ: *As the dark fog descended on him, he saw that fabled bird of Indian legend, which is born without feet and thus can never alight. It sleeps in the high winds and is only visible when it dies. When its transparent wings, longer than an eagle's, fold in, it fits in the palm of your hand.*

Let us summarize, then, what we know about Godard's mysterious Indian Bird of Death:

1. In *Bande à part*, Arthur sees this bird at the very moment of his death—just after he has been shot multiple times by his uncle, and Odile's face flashes before his eyes.

2. It's a bird, sharing certain universal bird characteristics such as wings, feathers, a beak, etc.

3. It's got an eagle-like wingspan, and we assume it is strong and an excellent flyer—while simultaneously fitting in the palm of your hand.

4. However, it's got no feet: it may never land nor rest but is doomed to fly forever.

5. The bird is Indian. This is where things gets complicated: India Indian or American Indian? Western men have been confused about this since the beginning of time.

6. Now, we enter the murky waters of guesswork and fabulation.

7. Is it a real bird—or at least based on an existing myth? Or did Godard make it up? How did an Indian bird find its way into this movie?

8. This bird suggests that my encounter with this movie is nothing shy of fate, of meant-to-be (*me, Indian boy; you, Indian bird; same same*).

9. Is this bird in fact an owl, a crow, a blackbird, or a cuckoo? An eagle, a ghostbird, or a frogmouth bird? A snakebird, or a Sterbekauz? But then, none of these would fit in the palm of my hand. And none of the above possess such magnificent transparent wings.

10. Some claim that the dead can watch us through the eyes of certain birds.

11. Why can we only see the bird when it dies? Don't we rather see it only when *we* die? Is this a mistake in the subtitles?

12. It's a Bird of Death, so I am imagining it is transporting the souls of the departed to . . . well, where exactly: another realm, a different time zone, the eternal winds,

Chandigarh, somewhere they will wait around to enter the next stage, to be reborn? How does the bird transport the souls? Does he carry them with his beak? Or does he swallow the souls whole to then spit them out again upon arrival? Does he digest them first? Are souls tasty? Transparent-spun-out-of-air tasty? I digress.

13. Would it be desirable to be carried by the Indian Bird of Death?

14. Are we allowed to choose whether he takes us or not?

15. Does it hurt?

FLY

Boarding a plane is the one thing I have never done in my life so far. Well, that and swimming and having sex. I do a lot of flying in my dreams, though. I board an actual airplane at Indira Gandhi International Airport. I've researched the best airlines in advance, so I'll know which plane to pick. The criteria for Best Airline are: the prettiest flight attendants, the softest free blankets, and, most importantly, the tastiest meals and in-between snacks. Flying to Europe via Doha seems to be a good choice. I dream of buying expensive oud scents with a golden credit card on my layover.

When I am strapped into my seat, looking out the window, seeing the engines lift and Delhi disappear, life feels crisp and pristine.

Things are in order, following a clear direction. Beyond the thick layer of smog, the sun is always shining. We know that much about plane travel, that the weather is always better up in the sky.

I close my eyes, leaning into the plush upholstered seat, engines running—and wake up on my charpoy with a start, knocking my foot into the wooden frame, feeling deflated. I always wake up before the plane can cross the very first border.

COLUMBIA

Oh—good day to you, Columbia.

Dressed like a Roman goddess, standing tall and proud on a pedestal amidst lush reddening clouds, Columbia is the United States personified as a woman—comparable to the British Britannia, Italian Italia Turrita, French Marianne, Indonesia's Ibu Pertiwi and our very own Bharat Matha, Mother India, often depicted in a saffron-colored sari standing on a lotus, holding a national flag and accompanied by a lion.

In several depictions, Europe is shown as a culturally refined lady, surrounded by a palette, a globe, and maps, standing opposite her freedom-loving counterpart Columbia. Even if their outfits and vibes are different, their faces appear almost identical—as if they are two different roles both played by the same actress, who has to change quickly in between scenes.

EUROPE: RE: YOUR RECENT INVITATION

This time I'm surprised to see the voice attached to a body. A tall woman with long, dark, wavy hair framing a milky-white face and striking violet eyes. She wears a white blouse, tucked into a skirt of the brightest blue. Her chair is poufy, cloud-like. Or is it an actual cloud? I cannot tell. She looks so clean and businesslike, I feel a bit disorderly in her presence.

"Good day, Happy Singh! I am contacting you regarding your recent invitation. Have you had a chance to reflect on our proposal?"

"Good day! So, this is the real deal, yes? This isn't a hoax?"

"A hoax? I should think not. What would give you that idea?"

"Well. It seems . . . surreal? To say the least. Surreal but nice, of course."

"A welcome surprise, I should hope. I love that scene in *Notting Hill*, by the way."

"Me, too. When he offers the apricots in honey . . . Have you ever had apricots in honey?"

"No, I must confess—"

"Me neither. I'd love to try it, though. Is it a well-known delicacy in Europe?"

"Possibly in Greece . . . You know what, now that the reception is crystal-clear, I think we should have a proper introduction. I am Europe, newly appointed Senior Recruiter in the Department of New Arrivals (Irregular and Regular), and your assigned coordinator for the journey—should you decide to accept our invitation. I have just been promoted, you see."

"Pleased to meet you. And hearty congratulations from my end! I am Happy, Happy Singh Soni. I do have a question, Miss Europe: why was I chosen?"

"That's easy enough to answer. You seem like the perfect fit. Cultured, refined, ambitious, fluent in foreign languages . . ."

"Stop it, you're making me blush."

"You're welcome. I am just summarizing the facts."

"Thank you. But I can't be the only one . . ."

"No, you're not the only one. I requested your case, in particular, though. I'm incredibly lucky to work with you."

"I am honored to be among the chosen ones. I will take some time to mull things over. It is—a life-changing decision, if there ever was one. And there is the matter of the fee, too, not insubstantial . . ."

"Of course. I completely understand. Take all the time you need to RSVP—that is, until the end of next month. That would be the deadline. In the meantime, can I take a picture for our files? If all works out, we can use it for your travel documents."

"Oh, I'm not really . . . prepared for a picture today. Let me just . . ."

"Your hair looks fine. Natural. No need to smooth it."

"Yeah, but . . . let me just try to . . ."

"This is great—" [takes a picture].

"Oh, OK. Does it look all right?"

"Well . . . no, you are sort of squinting, mouth wide open. Let's try again!"

"OK."

"You need to hold your head straight, try to avoid weird angles. Also, no need to look so . . . alluring. This is not a proper portrait, just a very pragmatic . . . Yes, great. This will do."

"Oh, no, please, I look horrible."

"The biometric thingy does that to any face. Even the most beautiful ones, such as yours."

"Am I not symmetric enough as it is?"

"Oh, you are quite symmetric, except that your whole head seems to be a bit . . . slanted? Have you never noticed?"

"Oh boy. Really? The biometry takes care of it though?"

"Yes, absolutely. Any further questions, Happy?"

"Yes, just one more: which airline will we be taking, should I decide to accept your invitation?"

"We will have to see about that. Whether via air or land, we will pick the most sensible route for you, and the agents will take care of the rest . . . no need to worry. Ah, I have a call on the other line, can you hold for a moment?"

"Sure."

"How do I get this thing to . . . Ever since they introduced the new system . . . Shall I just press here? Oh dear, I dropped the other call."

"If we go via air, will it be with Qatar? It's just, I've heard that the blankets they provide really are the best, as well as their selection of movies, and last but not least, the in-flight menu . . ."

"You know what, I'm not sure, Happy, but I am happy to check back and let you know. Ah, she is calling again. Sorry, will have to take this one. But you do have my email, yes? Feel free to contact me should you have any further concerns."

"Sure. Thank you! Tike, OK, bye."

THE FABLE OF THE CROW
AND THE WATER

Great things are bound to happen once you turn eighteen: sex and drugs and fame and magic.

For my eighteenth birthday I get a custom-made cream cake, rectangular, snow-white, and smooth like those plush well-made hotel beds you see on TV. It says *Happy Birthday Happy!* framed by sugary marigold garlands in electric green and gold.

Both my mother and my father tear off big chunks of cream cake with their hands and shove them into my mouth, before I even have my first sip of chai. A beloved Punjabi birthday tradition. Used to hate it as a kid; my jaw hurt because I had to keep my mouth open long enough so they could take a picture. But now I kind of like the customary cake-in-the-mouth shove.

After we finish the cake, my father tells me a story. I know it by heart; he has told it many times before. Babbu is famously reticent, except for when he's telling the fable of the crow and the water. He uses up all his words, like a river during monsoon, and then runs dry again. I try to listen as if it were the first time, but I drift off somewhere around the middle. All this cream is making me sleepy.

In a small village in northern Punjab, there once was a clever crow without a name.

How was the crow clever you ask?

Well, I will give you an example.

That summer was dazzlingly hot. It had been scorching for a while; temperatures had been rising since March, far too early. A drought befell the people in the village, who lived off rapeseed, potatoes, and cabbage, and the occasional skinny goat. Gargling rivers and trickling creeks all dried out. The earth cracked beneath the rotting corpses of small silver fish. Finally, even the wells dried up. There was no denying: the situation was desperate.

The nameless crow felt it, too. She hadn't had a sip of water in two days. Her throat was dry from the dead husks she fed off, and her little tongue gray rather than pink. Weakly, she landed on a small clay wall, separating a dried-out cabbage field from a farmer's compound. It was noon, the sun stood white and high, not a sound was to be heard. Everyone kept in the shade at this hour. Turning her black feathered neck, blinking her dry eyes, she spotted something glistening below. A jug, unmistakably filled with about an ounce of water.

The crow ticked her beak against the jug tentatively. It made a hollow sound. Feeling hope rise in her feathered chest, she grew a few inches taller. She peeked inside. Bowing over the rim of the jug, careful not to send it tipping and the precious water spilled on the gravel, she tried to reach the puddle at the bottom. The nameless crow stretched her neck as far as she could, but her beak couldn't reach the water.

The crow was getting frustrated. You might know the feeling.

Now, she fluttered over to a shady corner. She needed to think. She closed her eyes. Opened her eyes. She blinked a few times, crowed a few times, to remind herself who she was. She fluttered on the spot, stretching her wings tentatively. If she couldn't reach the water, the water needed to reach her—the conclusion was simple enough. But how to make the water rise and meet her beak?

Her gaze wandered. The small wall, separating farm and field, was framed by heaps of gravel and small rocks accumulating at its sides. The nameless crow had an idea. She flew down, jump, jump, jumped a few steps, eyed the rocks, and picked up some of the smallest stones with her beak. It seemed like a fruitless undertaking. Yet, bit by bit, she managed to fill the floor of the jug with little stones, adding layer upon layer, warding off dizziness as she jumped and flew.

The water rose with the stones. It pressed upwards, grayish and brown, tinged with dust, but water, nonetheless. Finally, her minuscule pink tongue could reach the glorious wetness, drop by drop, down down into her throat, into her heart, into her brain. Water. Her black marble eyes began to shine again. She looked up into the blaring sun, then stretched her neck again and finished the water. The rain, it came not long after that.

In the midst of this historic drought, of which countless men, women, children, and animals died, the crow survived thanks to the gifts of inventiveness and patience. Grit and endurance and using your brain instead of your muscles—these are important skills to remember in times of distress, my son.

This is how Babbu always ends the story, with some advice for me, which varies in wording but remains the same in its essence.

WONDERLAND GROUP CHAT: TERMINATION OF AGREEMENT

KING (PRIVATE MESSAGE): have u heard?

HAPPY (PRIVATE MESSAGE): what?

KING (PRIVATE MESSAGE): satish just got fired

HAPPY (PRIVATE MESSAGE): OK–shit. I mean, he's kind of a jerk. still.

MANAGER D: @WLTEAM general team meeting next tuesday. 7 p.m. after work. make sure u r on time

EUROPE IS PAINTING A PICTURE

"I am going to paint a picture, Happy. A picture of your life in Europe. In color and all. Ready? I am actually going to paint. You see? Brought my watercolors. New strategy from the Department of Brainstorming and Vision-Making. Picture this: a tree. A big tree. Let's say . . . an oak, OK? A tree in front of a house, planted on a juicy lawn. See, here. Nice and lush. Gonna use this lovely color, Maigrün they call it—it's a bit dried up, hand me the water—OK, now we've got a proper explosion of green. Luscious yet orderly, right? Humans need a little bit of order to coexist. Lesson number one, you can note that down: structure and order enable coexistence."

"OK, wait, wait, I didn't know I was supposed to note things down. I just thought you were going to paint a picture. Let me get my notebook. You don't happen to have a pen?"

"No, sorry, I just brought along my watercolors today. Why don't you use watercolor to write?"

"Like in calligraphy? I am not sure I am proficient in this ancient art . . ."

"No, just . . . You know what, I will summarize the bullet points for you later."

"Cool. Thanks."

"Yes, no problem, but let's continue, OK? Don't wanna lose momentum here. I was feeling inspired."

"OK then! You need a few more leaves up here in the tree, though. And the trunk could be a little more . . . knotty, you know. More old-looking. Like it belongs. Like generations and generations had inhabited that house before me. What does the house look like?"

"Uh—it's white. Big, white, sturdy, well-insulated . . . stone."

"What kind of stone?"

"Granite?"

"Is granite white though? It's rather grayish, isn't it. Only, can it be pink sandstone instead? I like pink sandstone."

"Well, yeah, of course it can. Pink sandstone it is. You normally wouldn't find pink sandstone in a European house, though."

"We have pink sandstone here, plenty of pink sandstone in Delhi."

"Yes, only . . ."

"Is granite superior to pink sandstone?"

"Not in any way, no, just, granite might be more stable . . ."

"If we're talking about stability, wouldn't steel be the thing? A house of steel. A house like a bullet. Can't imagine any love in a house of steel, though, can you?"

"You know what, let's put a pin in the stone-question and circle back to it later."

"Agreed. What about windows?"

"Sure, we got windows, too—big, stable windows. Well-insulated. French-looking. Elegant. See?"

"OK, I like that. What color is the door?"

"Hmm—green. That's an adequate color for a door, right?"

"Bit predictable. How about purple?"

"Do you think pink sandstone and a purple door—good idea?"

"No, you're right. That might clash. Yellow then. Bright yellow. That's a good combination if ever there was one. But then, we haven't properly decided on the stone question yet, have we?"

"True. You know what, Happy, our time is already up for today. Let's continue during our next meeting, shall we?"

AN EFFICIENT MAN'S MORNING ROUTINE

On the day of his death Davinder was thirty. The King of Hearts, the master of fairy lights. His star sign was Libra, Scorpio rising, and he was an electrician, a light technician, the best in town, maybe even in the whole north of India. His specialty was weddings. Intricate, Bollywood-level lighting. His lighting was a work of art, a symphony, really; so boasted the motto painted on his van. He was swamped the whole wedding season. Some brides booked him because he was easy on the eyes—looking pretty buff in his white T-shirts and always in his "lucky" leather sandals. Even the sandals looked cool on him.

All his customers walked away happy. He was a fun guy to be with. He had this way of slapping men on the shoulder, giving them a firm and reassuring pat, meaning, *All will be well. Don't worry, pal.* And they didn't. People believed him. I always believed him, too.

When Davinder hugged you, he really hugged you. His hands were always warm. Maybe because he was handling all that electricity.

I've always wondered: when you wake up on the day you're going to die, can you feel it? Is there such a thing as a premonition, a tingling sensation in your bones? Or do you simply go about your daily business and—swoosh! Lifeline cut off like a piece of meat under a sharp, shiny butcher's knife.

They told us it was a heart attack. While working a fancy city wedding, Davinder fell from an extendable ladder, four meters deep into an artfully trimmed bush of white oleander. Dead before he hit the ground. His legs sprawled like a starfish's, eyes wide-open.

When Davinder got up on the day he died, on a foggy December morning, he felt a bit weaker than usual, but assumed it was because of hockey practice the night before. But that didn't stop him from completing his usual routine: fifty push-ups, fifty sit-ups, thirty squats, a thirty-minute run around the fields.

I'd heard Davinder return from his run and accept a tea from Gul, talking quietly. I was too tired to get up just yet; I had a few more moments to savor between night and day, enveloped by the clatter and scents of the kitchen, the heat of my body inside my blanket keeping the winter chill at bay. After a quick shower, Davinder assembled his toolbox and heaved huge packages of extra-large and durable fairy lights into the van. Then he drove off to Jalandhar for his big gig.

THE GROOM IS A HEDGEHOG

The soon-to-be-wedded couple had been a funny one. Allegedly, the bride resembled the beautiful actress Deepika Padukone, while the groom looked like a hedgehog. A hedgehog ran over multiple times. But this hedgehog had made a small fortune with a mobile phone credit company, and he had a great sense of humor. That was all it took to marry a Deepika Padukone look-alike, it seemed.

This odd pairing made me think of a sentence in a tattered French textbook from the '60s that I'd found at Mr. Tuli's: *la mariée est une femme et le marié est un hérisson.* The bride is a woman, and the groom is a hedgehog. I'd always assumed it was a very stupid typo. Apparently, though, it's a thing: women, at times, are into hedgehogs.

I imagine Davinder arriving on the morning of the wedding, a hustling, bustling scene of anticipation. Service personnel populate the villa like ants, carrying plates of rose sweets underneath sheets of foil, buckets of pristine crushed ice, and heaps of marigold garlands. Meanwhile, musicians are already warming up in the snow-white party tent. The trumpet is seemingly off tune, but that's the way it's supposed to be. Why do Hindi wedding orchestras always sound so sad?

Davinder waves to the doorman, parks the van beside the oleander bushes, and sighs a raspy sigh. He lights a cigarette, coughs, and spits a nodule of mucus out of the open car window. It lands in the freshly dug-up earth. Indian roses are to be planted any minute; the gardener is already carrying them over from the shed in big boxes.

Davinder gets out his phone and texts the bride, aka Deepika: *I'm here.*

His phone pings. She's sent a heart emoji and a crying face in reply.

You see, it is very possible—I am almost one hundred percent sure—that Davinder and Deepika had been having an affair. It turned out they'd gone to elementary school together. But then Deepika's parents got moderately rich selling air-conditioning units, moving the family away to Chandigarh—and moving up in the world, to the comforts of the middle class. Davinder and Deepika hadn't seen each other in years, not until she hired him to do the lights. At that first meeting—discussing color schemes under the supervision of the clueless hedgehog—they couldn't keep their eyes away from each other. The next time, they met alone at the light suppliers. Surrounded by a thousand light bulbs in a small, enclosed space, the tension must have been palpable . . .

A kiss. It was only a kiss. But of course, it was much more than a kiss. Giving in, letting go, renouncing rules to be abided and vows to be given. Another skin to press and be pressed by. I might be getting carried away. We will give them some privacy and jump to the next bit.

They managed the coming meetings gracefully, never letting on, never getting caught. Davinder joked heartily with the hedgehog, punctuating each sentence with an extra-firm pat on his shoulder, receiving a hedgehoggy smile in return. Davinder did feel bad. He liked the hedgehog, he really did. Even if you are up against fate itself, you should feel a little bad, shouldn't you?

Yet, across a table, or across a room even, Davinder could always smell Deepika's hair: the scent of soap and heliotropes. He could even smell it when she wasn't there. Everything about her was precious and clean. Her body was straight and athletic; she would have outrun the hedgehog many times. She had a slight gap between her front teeth and a barely perceptible lisp, which made her even more adorable. Highly disciplined and eager to succeed, Davinder had been her only slip-up, ever.

Davinder starts to text back: *I* . . .

He is stuck after *I*.

He pauses, takes a drag of his cigarette, and blows smoke out the side of his slightly parted lips.

Then a second text from Deepika arrives: *Meet me on the roof.*

He shuts his phone (an old Motorola, the emojis still looks like this: <3 (;-;)). Pulling his heavy blue toolbox from underneath the seat, he opens the door. Throws the cigarette into the bushes. He pauses. It is significant that he pauses. He is not entering into this lightly. He unwraps a cheap minty chewing gum that loses its taste seconds after he's popped it in his mouth and goes up to the roof to meet her. He knows the way by heart.

How had Deepika reacted when she learned the news later that day? Had she kneeled beside him in the oleander bushes? Did she cry? Could she have attributed such a reaction to just a bit of a shock, the light technician dying on the day of your wedding? Had the hedgehog bought it?

Deepika and the hedgehog did get married in the end. On that day, however, no ceremony took place. It would have been considered unlucky. The rose sweets were given away to the maids, the marigold garlands wilted, the crushed ice melted. The band went home without having performed, and the service personnel shared sips of expensive whiskey in the tent before they disassembled it.

When I saw Deepika, two years later, on my way to watch a bad Hollywood movie in Model Town, she carried her small son on her arm. In my opinion, she didn't look anything like Deepika Padukone. I think her actual name was Chuni: one who is loved like a scarf you hold close to you.

FATEHPAL: INTERNATIONAL EXPERIENCE

"What was that YouTube video you sent me?"

"Ha, yeah—sorry. Greyson Chance singing 'Paparazzi' . . . I think . . . or the *MacGyver* cat? How you doing, Fatty?"

"Don't call me . . . It's Fatehpal. Seriously!"

"Sure, Fatehpalji. Sorry, sorry. I have a question for my clever eldest brother. The man with international experience."

"OK, shoot. No one's hailing a taxi tonight. Tuesday. Town's dead."

"So, you know, when you went abroad . . ."

"You were so small, ha. Tiny little thing."

"Yes, and you were still tiny, too . . ."

"What is that supposed to mean?"

"Just . . . last picture I saw . . ."

"What?"

"Well, a paunch is very common for the Indian man in middle age really . . ."

"Can't believe . . . the cheek . . . If I would have been around longer you wouldn't talk like this . . . They spoiled you. I told Gul. Raise him to be a proper man!"

"I am a man, dude! I'm eighteen!"

"Well, time will tell . . . Ah, drunk English tourists incoming. Oh boy . . . Take care, Happy."

"OK, can I call you another time? Tomorrow?"

"Sure, sure, brother. Tike, OK, bye."

WONDERLAND GROUP CHAT: BULLET POINTS

MR. CEO: @WLTEAM plz summarize your current duties and responsibilities in bullet point format

MANAGER D: bring document along for the team meeting.

KING (PRIVATE MESSAGE): what's bullet point format?

HAPPY (PRIVATE MESSAGE): no worries. I can write yours for you, easy: - cotton candy making - cotton candy selling - customer relations.

KING (PRIVATE MESSAGE): thanks, man . . . you've earned yourself all-you-can-eat cotton candy for life . . .

EUROPE: A FRIENDLY REMINDER

"Have you had the chance to think about your invitation to Europe, Happy? This is a friendly reminder that you have two months left to decide."

"Hi, Europe. I have, yes. Read most of it, I think. Though the print is very small at times. I wonder if I do need glasses . . ."

"And have you come to a decision?"

"Yes. I do want to go. I am almost entirely one hundred percent sure."

"Oh, I'm glad to hear. Congrats. You won't regret it. Have you signed the agreement yet?"

"Not yet. I just have to get the fee together first. I am close, though. Not long until I reach the target sum."

"Oh, well, this gives you plenty of time to prepare. Polish up your language skills, hone your soft skills, read up on intercultural competences, et cetera."

"Yes, great—will I be honing my skills on my own or is there a program I could join?"

"Well, we do have a module on intercultural competences we offer at the Department of Arrivals, yes. Let me check. It is slightly . . . let's say, outdated, but the core ideas should still come across. I believe there is a funny video on the misunderstandings that can arise from the Indian head nod . . ."

"OK. Well, I, personally won't be needing that video in particular, but thanks for looking into it. Would be great if I could join. Also in order to meet my fellow travelers."

"Ah, it's more of a video course you will be able to complete in your own time. I will look into the matter and let you know. Any further questions, Happy?"

"Nothing else so far. I'll let you know if anything comes to mind, though. Yes—actually, one thing: food-wise, what will I expect during the journey? Is there a menu? I love menus. Love to plan."

"Ehm—I am not sure there is a menu. It might be more of a seasonal, regional, day-to-day kind of thing. Let me check though. I will get back to you."

BE A MAN, GO ABROAD: KARAMVEER SINGH'S TRAVEL AGENCY

BECOME WHO YOU ARE MEANT TO BE!
EUROPE, USA, GET READY, HERE I COME!
BE A GOOD MAN, GO ABROAD.
Ring-ring—who's there?—Your future!
Don't sit around and wait for your life to happen.

Offering full-complete-total-all-around-carefree packages,
in-depth consulting,
and worry-free arrangements—call NOW,
come by TODAY,
leave TOMORROW.

THE NEW JERSEY BOTS

I search for the hashtag Jalandhar and scroll down as far as I can. Most images are photos of girls: girls in pastel-colored salwar kameez, or in jeans and tight black T-shirts, leaning against cars and walls. Girls in shopping malls or looking out toward a river in longing. One girl is sitting by the concrete stairs of a villa, looking sober and kind; a school portrait kind of smile. Another woman made up like a Bollywood star with pointy white shoes and blown-out hair, sitting on a white swing. Her name is Jassy Deol: Nursing Girl, Ziddy Girl, Chocolate Lover. Her dream is to live in New Jersey. She is five feet seven without heels. Looking at her feed, Jassy Deol seems to be not one woman, but many: a shapeshifter, she takes on various faces, bodies, outfits, styles; an amalgam of Punjabi girlness. They all want to go to New Jersey. They are all five feet seven without heels.

I feel I need to get to the bottom of this, so I send a direct message to Jassy Deol.

@happyTV: Hi Jassy! Hope you are well! Just wondering: why do you mention your height without heels? And why do you want to go to New Jersey?
Many thanks for your reply.
Kindly,
Happy Singh

@JASSY_DEOL: Hi gorgeous! How are you today?

@happyTV: I'm good, thanks. How are you?

@JASSY_DEOL: Amazing! You look hot in your picture.
Are you lonely sometimes?
I am lonely sometimes. :((((Greetings from Dubai.

@happyTV: Oh, I thought you were a Jalandhar girl.

@JASSY_DEOL: I am everywhere, darling. I can see you in my dreams. Do you like the ocean?

@happyTV: I have never been, to be honest. I must confess, I cannot swim.

@JASSY_DEOL: I can be a dolphin if you want me to be.

@happyTV: Oh, great. I mean, you don't have to turn yourself into a dolphin just for me. You can just be who you want to be.

@JASSY_DEOL: Sometimes it's all a bit much.

@happyTV: Oh yeah, I feel you. Workwise, or romantically . . .

@JASSY_DEOL: I lack the necessary funds to lead the life I want to lead. No one is protecting me. Sometimes I am a bit lonely. :((((

@happyTV: I am so sorry to hear. Could we circle back to my initial question though: why do you want to emigrate to America so badly? And what do your heels have got to do with it?

@JASSY_DEOL: Lol. I like your sense of humor. You are a hunk. You just get me like no one else does. I am healing. I am alone in a forest. I think I am lost.

@happyTV Oh dear, this sounds rather . . . do you need any help?

@JASSY_DEOL: Yes, please. I lack the necessary funds to lead the life I want to lead.

@happyTV: I thought you were lost in a forest.

@JASSY_DEOL: Please transfer the aforementioned amount onto the following Paypal account: jessy.deol@honeylove.in

@happyTV: I think you might be in the wrong chat.

@JASSY_DEOL: Mehra Papa Jalandhar hu.

@happyTV: Yes, that's great—anyways, I wish you all the best and a very bright future! May you be showered with luck and happiness.

@JASSY_DEOL: Lol. I like your sense of humor. You are a hunk. Sometimes I am a bit lonely. :((((

EUROPE: FIRST ADMONITION

"Good day, Happy."

"It is three in the morning. More like, g'night."

"I must have miscalculated the time difference. I apologize. Lots of time zones in my cal. This is a kind reminder that you have one week left to decide."

"Yes, I know, thank you."

"Anything to aid you with your decision?"

"I'd say I'll sleep on it, but then . . ."

"Sorry again. I just have to stick to the schedule, you see—the rhythm of reminders is preset, I can't change it."

"Of course. No worries. As I mentioned before, I am super honored to be given this opportunity . . ."

"I completely understand. Do take this last week to decide—and use it well. I always recommend a good old pro and con list. I wish I could be of further assistance, but the decision is up to you. Please contact me if there are any further questions."

GONNA FLY NOW

My head splits in two. Then the stairs of the Philadelphia Museum of Art emerge inside the incision, and Sly is running up to the top of my brain, pumping his fists in the air.

Suddenly the hold music stops, and the hotline gives a beeping sound. The voice of a sober old lady greets me in an accent that I can't quite place.

"My name is Happy Singh Soni. I am calling from Wonderland. I bumped my head on a steel rod on the Rocky Ride. I think I briefly hallucinated. Am I dying?"

"Good day. What is the reason for your call, sir? I couldn't catch that just now, apologies."

"I bumped my head, quite hard. Will I die? What do you reckon?"

"I see. Most likely not. Not yet. Statistically. Let me ask you a few questions:"—she shuffles for a piece of paper and reads—"Do you feel a pounding pain in your head? Is your vision blurred?"

"Yes. And yes."

"OK. Are you bleeding?"

"No. Not as far as I can see."

"Are you bleeding through your nose?"

I feel for liquid inside my nose. It tickles. I sneeze.

"No."

"Are you nauseous? As in, do you feel sick rising up into your mouth, do you need to vomit?"

"Yes, a little bit is rising up as we speak. And my head really hurts. I can't see properly. You see, Sylvester Stallone keeps running up the stairs in my head. Pretty distracting. It was a *solid* steel rod."

"OK, OK. Well, why don't you come down for an examination right now, so we can have you checked out? We partner with Sacred Heart Hospital for our privately insured patients."

"I'm afraid I can't leave my shift."

"If you are on the Level C Green scheme, I am also able to give you a medical consultation via phone. Are you insured over the Level C Green scheme? Or are you B Purple?"

"I am not entirely sure."

"Do you have your insurance number at hand? I could check for you."

"I don't know where to find it."

"Did you get a card from Wonderland when you started your job? Blue, green, or purple?"

"Oh, yes, hold on—here you go: A Y HSS 19910930."

"Ah, I see. Hm. You are classified as A Yellow. Nothing I can do for A Yellow, I'm afraid. You shouldn't even have this number."

"OK. But—I'm confused. My manager gave me this number."

"He shouldn't have. Sorry, but I will have to terminate the call for data protection reasons. There are different rules for A Yellow. Good-bye, and best of luck."

"Wait, just a second! Hello?"

Disconnected. And then Sly is back again, running up the stairs, pumping his fists into my skullcap, making me forget who I am.

COOKIES AND DISINFECTANT

When I wake up, Ambika's face is looming over me like a moon sculpted of sandstone. It smells of cookies and disinfectant.

"You have given us such a scare, idiot." She smiles a quick smile, barely noticeable to the untrained eye, and gives my sweaty head a pat.

I look around. My skull hurts when I try to turn it. I close my eyes. Sly is gone. I open my eyes again. Everything in the room is beige and pink. Who will pay the hospital bill? Guiltily, I think about my life savings in the empty barfi box underneath my bed, labeled *Europe Funds*.

The tall figure of Babbu Singh enters the room carefully; shy in the formal environment of the hospital. He's known to shed a tear easily, and he does so now, as he embraces me.

"Happy." He holds my head up between his two big hands so he can look at me, and it hurts a little.

"Hello, Papaji." I smile and groan. In his eyes, I am still the little one, and I always will be.

"I will leave you two to it." As Ambika gathers her things in a new tote bag made from soft black leather, she presses a pink Post-it with a name and a number in my hands, in Gul's green script. "Before I forget, this guy called for you at home. Do you know what this is about?"

"Um . . . not sure. Thanks, though. Will call back."

It scares me a little to lie to her, I must confess, but the fear feels spacious: like it could house a whole new life.

FRANZ AND ODILE
DECIDE TO LEAVE

Franz and Odile have had enough. You can only dance a dance so many times. Only plan a heist, kiss and plot and hatch and hide, run through the Louvre, keep one minute of silence, disappear, and begin anew, before ennui begins to arise. Ennui, no, we can't have that. Ennui will lead to purposelessness, will lead to depression, and will result in certain death. Franz and Odile do not want to die. The tension, the rapt tension of an arc unfolding, it needs to be kept alive. So, Franz and Odile decide to vary their lines. Only tiny adjustments at first: *maybe* instead of *yes*, *yes* instead of *maybe*. Odile takes off her black velvet bow and fastens a white one to her hair instead. Of no consequence to the overall plot. Barely perceptible to the untrained ear and eye, to someone who hasn't watched this movie many times over.

But yes, it is true: our heroes are plotting their escape.

MON HISTOIRE COMMENCE ICI

It's time. I've had the agent's number forever. Written down on the pink Post-it, crumbled and humid. I take it out of my left jean pocket. I dial the number. I force myself to be firm, channeling some good old Punjabi masculinity. The voice on the other end sounds tinny and bored. He coughs and spits audibly before he replies, probably smoking an unfiltered cigarette. I get what I need, without embellishments: the date and the amount. I am to bring the exact fee in cash for the date of the collection. Just one small bag.

A weeklong car journey through the Middle East, and into Europe. Can't be too bad, can it? I'll make friends along the way. There are bound to be bonding moments, crossing borders together and all.

The glory of a decision made. I want to shout it from the cluttered rooftops of our village, like six rockets shooting up at once: *I'm*

*leaving! Not on a jet plane! But! Bag is packed! Gone in a flash! Will
you miss me?*

I imagine bells ringing with the announcement, those tiny tingly
ones that some goats have strapped around their necks on leather
bands, and a herd of water buffaloes running up a hill, smiling
coyly, bursting into song: *Happy, Happy!* They fan out and wave
colorful silk scarves (with their snouts, possibly? They couldn't very
well use their hooves, could they?), signaling my departure, marking a new beginning.

WILL YOU MISS ME

When I finally tell her, Gul breaks into angry tears. Her face becomes
that of a four-year-old girl being refused a spoon of honey. She goes
off to clean the already clean kitchen and makes a lot of noise while
doing so.

Babbu remains silent. In fact, he does not react at all for what
feels like a few minutes. Finally, he speaks:

"And upon arrival . . . what are your plans, son? Have you thought
this through?"

I have. The first step will be to attend as many castings as I can.
I know you need an agent, but that will be hard to facilitate initially.
The next step will be to make contacts and mingle. To polish up my
English, French, and Italian skills. Of course, I will have to take on a
day job to make ends meet: to pay off the debt to the coordinators
and send some money back home to my parents, as one does.

Gul returns, clasps her hands over her chest, and closes her eyes. The intricate network of wrinkles connecting her heavy lids to her full cheeks expresses the scope of the situation most expertly.

"Say something, Babbu. Tell him. For once in your life, speak!"

Babbu puts his cup of tea down.

The perpetual sadness behind his mole-like glasses grows large and mighty, and finally spills over. I become an empty vessel. Briefly, the vastness of his pain fills me entirely, surging up into my lips, my hair, my fingertips. My knees become wobbly. I crouch down and hug him like I did when I was a little boy. His glasses askew, he returns the embrace. My wet face presses into his forever red turban, smelling of Mysore sandalwood and ghee. Gul mutters an inaudible prayer. Her breathing is heavy and loaded. I close my eyes. Seven days to go.

AUTOBAHN

Ambika takes me for a ride: a farewell day-trip kind of thing. Officially, we are going to Amritsar, to get blessings for my journey to Europe. In actuality, we are driving to Delhi, taking the multiway motorways to get golgappas and see the sun rise in Lodi Gardens. My going away party isn't a party, but a trip clandestine.

I love her husband's big car, a Tata Aria SUV. I feel safe in here. Insulated. It even has a digital concierge who asks you things like, *Shall I turn up the AC? Are you hot? Are you cold?*

Ambika and I start to giggle when the voice asks, *Are you hot?*

"Damn right I am," she says, shaking back her hair like the Pantene girls do.

The road is rocky and dusty to start with. The streets become straighter and smoother once we enter Haryana. She goes faster, looking serious. I know this look. She is in the zone. The smog is already thick, and it gets even denser as we progress toward the city. You can barely make out the dim lights of the other cars on the road. The motorway is rather empty, but still. I'm a bit worried but try to play it cool. To diffuse the tension, I start to giggle, holding on the door handle tightly.

"Ambika! That's enough. Seriously."

She turns to me and smiles.

"Leave me in peace. I know what I'm doing."

"Think of Amanjot! You want her to grow up without a mother?"

"Oh, come on!"

"How did you even get your husband to let you go away alone for the weekend?"

"Who says I need someone to allow me to leave."

"Autobahn" by Kraftwerk is blaring from the car speakers. The song is endless. It goes on for about twenty minutes. All this time, she doesn't take her foot off the gas pedal. Have you ever sped over a Delhi motorway, immersed in a haze of dense January smog, listening to Kraftwerk? I would strongly recommend you try it before you die.

"Are you happy, Happy?"

Ambika suddenly touches my arm, taking her hand off the steering wheel, briefly.

"Are you really sure you want to leave?"

Panipuri has many names: fuchka or gupchup or golgappa or pani ke patake. My favorite name is golgappa. The very best golgappas are to be found at Rasili Chaat in Delhi's south. This is why we've come to Delhi after all: to taste the very best golgappas. As many as we can eat. You can never just have one, but always many; three at least. There are proper golgappa competitions, sponsored by Tata Motors, and the current record is fifty golgappas in one sitting, gobbled up by a man from Gujarat.

When we arrive, we are so tired, we almost don't muster up the strength to eat. Finding a place to park is an insane task alone. Driving through the city is madness. In the queue we poke each other to keep our eyes open. People shove us aside to get to the front of the line, but Ambika puts them in their place with her eyes, and when that doesn't work, she uses her pointy elbows.

Golgappas: small balls of dough, fried until they blow up in perfect bubbles, crisp and golden. Inside they are hot and hollow, filled with a spicy mash of potatoes and peas. Drizzled with sweet mango chutney and tamarind-mint sauce, the whole thing unfolds in your mouth like a sunrise in Lodi Gardens, when the smog isn't obscuring the light. Say the word *golgappa*, turn it around on your tongue, and you can imagine the taste. I eat nine golgappas and Ambika manages eleven; we down them with three huge cups of water with sugar cane and lime, and then take a nap in the car, fast asleep like well-fed babies.

I PACK MY BAG AND IN IT I PUT

1. a travel size bottle of Amla hair oil

2. a packet of Magic Masala Crisps

3. the Godard VHS collector's edition

4. one of Gul's chunnis (a bright yellow one with golden embroidery)

5. my lucky "dancing" shoes: adidas last frontier with blue stripes

6. the notebooks containing my favorite screenplays and two empty ones for new European writing

7. a gulmohar blossom in a sealed plastic bag

8. an unripe guava, which I hope will be perfect once I arrive in Europe

DAVINDER'S ROOM

An autographed photo of Bruce Lee is stuck into the frame of a half-blind mirror. It's not a portrait but a movie still; I don't know from which one. He has slashes all over his left cheek and his chest is bare. He is licking the fingers of his right hand. A peculiar gesture.

Davinder had gotten it off eBay. The signature is pretty cool: slanted, elegant, with the line of the L going off all billowy and providing a bed for the two E's. I wonder whether it's authentic. But if Davinder believed it was the real thing, then it is.

I remember when Davinder showed me Bruce Lee's "Lost Interview" from 1971. I search for it on my phone and press play.

PIERRE BERTON: What does he choose: the East or the West? This is a question most budding movie actors would welcome. This episode comes to you from Hong Kong. Our guest is the man who taught karate, judo, and chinese boxing to James Garner, Steve McQueen, James Coburn, and many more. The Mandarin Superstar—and he doesn't even speak Mandarin! His name is Bruce Lee. He's here today with a message for Happy Singh Soni, who is about to embark on a major adventure, with a similar question in mind: Will he find success in Europe? Bruce, welcome. If you could give one piece advice to our young aspiring artist, what would it be?

BRUCE LEE: You see, to me, a motion picture is *motion*. You gotta keep the dialogue down to the minimum. However, it is essential that you keep moving. You know? Nothing truly powerful can be achieved if you only stay in one place.

PIERRE BERTON: And what is the way to go about it? *How* will Happy Singh make it in Europe?

BRUCE LEE: The way to go about it is practice. Constant practice. Practice without a specific goal in mind. I had no idea that the martial arts I was studying would eventually lead to all of this. But I stuck with it. Every single day. Martial arts have a very deep meaning as far as my life is concerned, because, as an actor, as an artist, as a human being—all things I have learned from martial arts. It is, in short, the art of expressing the human body. In a way, it is learning acting by *un*-acting.

PIERRE BERTON: You have lost me.

BRUCE LEE: I mean, what I am saying is, here is the natural instinct. And here is control. You are to combine the two in harmony. The ideal is . . . natural unnaturalness, or unnatural naturalness.

PIERRE BERTON: Yin yang, eh?

BRUCE LEE: Exactly, man, that's it . . .

I pull the postcard out of the mirror's frame and slide it into the side pocket of my backpack, next to my passport and a bundle of rupee bills from my barfi box's savings account. I think Davinder would have liked me to have it.

KNOW EVERY THINGS

GUL

I remember when you were five years old and very, very sick—so thin, so frail, no food stayed inside, you should've seen yourself, a tiny ghost the color of chickpea flour—and Karamveer Kaur, she told me, "This boy is not gonna make it. Too weak!" This she told me, to my face, as I was praying, day and night, night and day, not sleeping. I never slept. And I replied, while burning incense over your little head, giving it a proper twirl, and praying to Guru Nanak Ji, "He will make it. He may not be strong outside, but he is mighty on the inside. Happy is my son after all."

You are my son. Be proud. Be strong. Be a Soni. Yes? Promise me.

This movie star thing—put it out of your mind. Like this [mimicking a folding motion with her hands, as if she were packing away the dress of a tiny doll], put it in a little box for safekeeping. Look at it from time to time. Be happy you have many ideas. Life will never be boring for you. But, please, choose a practical profession. Something you can hold in your hands. Something that feeds you, and feeds others. Everyone needs food, son. Stick to where the food is.

Take this image of Guru Nanak and put it up for your prayer—and don't lose it. You keep losing things. Have you packed your bag? A proper bag? No flimsy plasticy nonsense. Your documents? Underwear? Take enough underwear to change. Take some medicine also.

Here, here. No, you need it, of course, it is essential: Nurofen, cur-
cumin, brahmi for peace of mind, and some antibiotics. Expired, but
still fine. You never know. Better be prepared. Always be prepared.
And eat, boy, eat.

BABBU

I am not one for many words.

Just know this:

Don't look at what other people do; do what you do. And think.
Think for yourself. Don't think the thoughts of others, think your own.

And if you are unsure which direction to turn, look at the crows
for advice. They will tell you if you listen closely.

AMBIKA

Once you leave, that's it. You've made the decision. Don't look behind
you, or change directions, it will just split you in two: one part always
here, one part always there. Nothing new can ever grow when you
are split in two. I do love you, stupid. You wouldn't even know.

FATEHPAL

And even if, along the way, it seems like it won't be well, it will still
be well in the end. You are lucky. I know you are.

Take some warm things. One of Gul's shawls. It might get cold in
Europe. Like, cold in a way you think might end your life. But it won't!
Don't worry. And one last thing: In some situations, it's good to keep
your mouth shut. Pretend you don't know even if you do. You know
that you know. No one can take that away from you. Let this be
enough. And call me if you get in trouble, little brother.

SOME RANDOM DUDE AT THE MARKET SELLING
ME LADYFINGERS

Europe, eh? Italy? No, never wanted to go. Everyone wants to go, away, away. Now, if it's not Europe, it's America, it's Canada, it's even New Zealand.

I have my ladyfingers, my eggplants, my guavas, my stall, every time same things, every week same spot. I don't want big, big change. Always: elsewhere, elsewhere, elsewhere. Recipe to get unhappy. Where is your head? Where is your heart? Where is your ass when it's at home? Where is your mind, son, if you're always on the run? Never in one place, always many. I do keep up. Don't think I don't know what goes on in the world. I know things. But I don't need to know every things.

INTERMISSION: ON THE MOVE

SCENE 1, EXT.—DAWN

On the day of the departure, we meet in Jalandhar-east Tehsil next to Rama Electricals at 5 a.m.

The sun has not yet risen. The street light casts a yellow, flickering gleam, which makes a guy's skin look a little sickly. Not the best lighting setup for the first scene of my big break. Except for the two agents, smoking and looking at their phones, only one of my costars is already here waiting. He stands tall in a thick blue wool jumper and worker's cargo pants, eyes narrowed, arms crossed. In his perfectly wrapped turban, neatly groomed beard, and immaculate posture, he reminds me of a warrior king avatar from a computer game I used to play. For real, though, I feel like I've seen him before. Where do I know him from? When I greet him, he merely nods and closes his eyes again. I immediately feel minuscule. Washed out and shrunk; a delicate textile that's been put through the wrong cycle. Not the best start to my big adventure.

I open my backpack and unfold a sugared roti, the last delicious morsel of Gul's cooking I will eat for a long while, wrapped in alu foil and still warm from the tawa.

LOG OF TRAVELERS:
JALANDHAR-EAST TEHSIL

AMRIT PURI (*1990)
Republic of India
Type: P
Nationality: IND
Sex: M
Place of Birth: Kapurthala
Date of Issue: 18/04/2004

HAPPY SINGH SONI (*1991)
Republic of India
Type: P
Nationality: IND
Sex: M
Place of Birth: Jalandhar
Date of Issue: 01/09/2008

HARBIR SINGH BHARAJ (*1988)
Republic of India
Type: P
Nationality: IND
Sex: M
Place of Birth: Tajpur
Date of Issue: 22/08/2006

NADEESH NIHANG (*1992)
Republic of India
Type: P
Nationality: IND
Sex: M
Place of Birth: Kapurthala
Date of Issue: 22/08/2006

SUKHA DHILLON (*1986)
Republic of India
Type: P
Nationality: IND
Sex: M
Place of Birth: Jalandhar
Date of Issue: 12/12/2009

VASUDEV SINGH SARAI (*1991)
Republic of India
Type: P
Nationality: IND
Sex: M
Place of Birth: Hoshiarpur
Date of Issue: 13/03/2007

MARUTI SUZUKI OMNI (*1998)

Our van is a Maruti Suzuki Omni (current mileage: 612.732 km). I
think it used to be a fast-food truck. At the driver's door it still says
Wah Ji Rahul Chicken Centre and the seats smell like cold lard.

NO ONE

Clandestine travel is a lot simpler if you cross out your name on your passport and choose to become no one. No basic needs getting in the way of progress; for progress must be made, and time is money.

We are sitting close like sparrows puffing up their plumage amongst the thick knots of cables. Behind the dirty windows of the Suzuki Omni, a gauze of roadside dust, we are the veiled ones, passing from one state to another. Wave if you see us on the road, or far out at sea. Wave, stranger, as a greeting might help us to remember who we are.

We are a murmuration of birds, a murder of crows, a swarm, a plural entity; an idea, a tingling, a premonition, a complicated melody you cannot forget; and so, as per usual, you hum.

AMRIT AND NADEESH

I am sitting next to Amrit and Nadeesh, best friends from Kapurthala. They take turns playing each other songs on their mobile phones: "Electric Relaxation" by A Tribe Called Quest followed by "Chandigarh," the new single by Karan Jasbir and Yo Yo Honey Singh. They sing along. Amrit laughs like a guinea pig. Nadeesh's left eyebrow is shaved and the skin there is shiny—a scar from when he'd been working at the Crispy Hawker in Lambra and accidentally tipped over a boiling pot of oil. It's a miracle he hadn't gone blind.

You know, I think the scar will give me a bit of edge. Ladies love scars, he'd said to Amrit after they fired him.

Both Nadeesh's and Amrit's fathers owned takeout restaurants in Prakash Nagar, Jalandhar: chole kulche and vada pav, respectively. As a five-year-old, Nadeesh would hide underneath the counter, sorting the paper boxes his father used to serve the kulche. Loud noise and hubbub scared him, so he always stayed inside the neon-lit shop. He stacks them diligently, counting aloud (for he could count already), tongue sticking out in between his pink lips in concentration.

Amrit, meanwhile, had been watching him from the open door with a bhutta masala in hand. A social butterfly at the tender age of four and three-quarters, he'd been meaning to make contact for quite some time. So, after careful consideration, he marched inside and kicked over Nadeesh's tower of boxes with his brand-new trainers.

Instead of crying, Nadeesh had laughed. Amrit handed Nadeesh the buttery corncob, half-eaten, offering him the sleeve of his blue sweater to wipe off his fatty fingers after he'd finished eating. The stain never did come out, no matter how hard Amrit's mother scrubbed.

AISHWARYA RAI, AGAIN

When I open my eyes, Aishwarya Rai has materialized on the seat opposite of me. She looks sad. Her green irises grow, protrude, and fall onto the floor, where they morph into glistening amla fruit. They multiply quickly. Green Indian gooseberries are rolling around the floor of the van like shiny lacquered marbles. They transform into pickles and curries and oils, cooked by a magical, invisible hand, presenting themselves in an array of stainless-steel bowls hovering midair, a dance of great taste and vitamin C.

I look up into Aishwarya's eyes. They are perfect blanks, devoid of color.

LOCATE ME

My phone is too slow. Seems I've filmed too many videos for Happy TV. The storage is full, but I can't decide which videos to delete. The agents haven't told us much about the route. My phone has a compass and a map—even one for the sky, indicating stars and stellar constellations. I try to locate myself, but the map just keeps buffering.

HARBIR

I knew I'd seen Warrior King before IRL. Once, Harbir had repaired our century-old Mahindra tractor without uttering so much as a Sat Sri Akaal. I think I was thirteen at the time; he was only a couple of years older, but then as now, he'd towered over me like a tree over a marigold flower. I overheard Gul telling Ambika the village gossip after he'd left Soni Square, driving off in a spluttery pickup, pink palms marbled with black motor oil. Harbir was a mechanic, like his father—Daljeet Singh, of Daljeet Singh's Automobile Repairs in Tajpur. Harbir had taken over the business after his old man died of a stroke, but never bothered to change the name. Repainting the sign above the garage would have been too costly; besides, people had gotten used to it over the years. His mother needed hip surgery, his sisters needed to be married off— the burden to finance and arrange it all now lay on his shoulders alone. Gul had sighed while telling this story, as if she knew the feeling.

THE DESERT: DASHT-E LUT

The light has changed. I look at my phone and check the blue dot hovering along the map: this is me :), in the middle of a light brown nothing. We have crossed into desert territory.

Dasht-e Lut: the hottest desert in the world. But it is January, and the sky is covered by thickset clouds; a sky like a wall, I think, as I glance through the dirty windows of the van. The motor has been turned off and the white noise of the road is gone. The agents have left their front seats. Lut means "bare and empty" in Persian. A rippling surface of saline beds. High and low planes, barren and beguiling. Incessant motion, even if we don't see it now, and the earth seems perfectly still, asleep. Old dunes, new dunes. No destruction, just becoming.

I tilt my head so I can see farther outside the window. Far out at the horizon, I can see tall rock formations—Kalouts. They look like they've been dropped into this world from a far-off planet. There is a fissure in the clouds, and, very briefly, the magnanimous rocks are bathed in milky orange light.

The agents get back in the van and bring with them the scent of tobacco and an air of concern. The Suzuki ignites. The tires have a hard time managing the sandy road. The motor howls. Nadeesh rubs his eyes in his sleep and jams an elbow into my side. It feels like we are driving back the same way we came. When I try to check the map again, it tells me there is no device detected.

Time passes like sand trickling through an irregularly shaped glass, and I can't put my finger on the hour.

A VERY TALL MAN

A man is wandering by the side of the dusty track. He must be over two meters tall, and his legs go up to the sky. Who would walk by the road in the middle of nowhere? He comes closer and steps into the flicker of the road stall's light. His head is wrapped in a mud-colored turban. He is sipping guava juice from a Tetra pak and carries a bag made from straw. He nods at me and smiles.

"Good evening," I reply. "Would you like some chips to go with your juice?"

"Ha. OK. Yes, thank you. Are you always this kind to strangers?"

He inclines his head slightly and fishes out some last crumbs from the bag I hold out to him.

"I just haven't seen anyone new in a long while. Except for my current travel companions. We are going through a rough patch, to be honest. I could use some outside perspectives."

"I see. What is your name?"

"Happy. Happy Singh. Pleased to meet you."

"I am Knut. My pleasure."

"Where are you headed?"

"Chicken Street No. 1 in Kabul."

"Oh. OK. That's a precise address. Why Chicken Street?"

"That's the place where Alighiero e Boetti had his One Hotel. Long time ago. Let's say I'm a fan of his work."

"That . . . sounds interesting! Are you walking all the way?"

"I will take the bus later. No worries. I am not insane."

"Who was this Boetti guy? I must admit, I do not know of him."

"Yeah, sorry. You don't have to know him. He was an Italian art-ist. He liked being a host. Inviting people. This is why he opened a hotel in Kabul. This is a personal pilgrimage, if you will."

"Wow, OK, cool. I am on a pilgrimage, too. Well, not really. I am on my way to Europe. I am looking forward to having a house to invite people to."

"Where in Europe are you headed?"

"Anywhere, really. But the first stop is Italy."

"OK. Well. That is quite an undertaking. Are you scared?"

"No. A little bit, maybe. I hope the worst is over already. I would just love to know the future. It would give me strength."

"I understand. I feel the same. Unfortunately, I cannot tell the future. But . . . I can read your palm, if you like?"

"Oh. Cool. My mother used to read palms, but she rarely does it anymore."

"Shall I have a look?"

"Yeah, sure, OK , go ahead."

"OK. Yeah. I can see something. A few things, actually . . .

"First, you will grow intimate with beings that once lived out at sea. You will touch them, many times. Then, you will help things grow. You will also meet your very best friend, dressed in dungarees.

"And then . . . something will happen that separates you from the world.

"From then on, I cannot see your future clearly. But I can see a hill and a wiiiiiiide sky. And a funny-looking dog. Or is it a sheep?

"Ha. I cannot tell for certain. A furry animal in any case will be your companion for a while."

"You can see all this? Wow. I don't quite . . . This is all in my palm?"

"Yes."

"I don't know whether I got everything right, but . . ."

The van honks—slightly off tune, capturing collective exhaustion in a single accord. Harbir calls my name, already annoyed by my lateness, which isn't, I admit, a rarity. I tend to linger at roadside stalls. I turn to him and wave, signaling I'll be there in a bit.

"OK, I gotta run. They will leave without me if I don't hurry. But thank you so much. Seriously. This was—"

"My pleasure." He bows down slightly. "Good luck to you, my friend. Hold on to that natural exuberance of yours, it will come in handy."

"OK, ha, I will. Safe travels to you! Have fun with, well . . . the ghost of Boetti."

THE VALUE OF HIGH-QUALITY WATER BOTTLES

The scent of pee in plastic fills the van like a polluted undercurrent, pungent and abiding. We pee in empty plastic bottles until they are filled to the brink, threatening to spill. You have to screw the lid on tightly. But cheap bottles don't close properly. Suffice to say, there is always spilled piss on the ground, floating between our sneakers. I brush my arm against my nose. My skin carries a faint residue of rice and ghee, the smell of our dark living room back in Soni Square.

PLAY DEAD

Arthur is falling. Tripping, staggering, stumbling—still standing, though, still walking. One, two, three—now, he pulls the trigger once more. Twice more. Thrice. *Shoot! Boom! Paff!*

Now Arthur has collapsed onto the ground. His body twitches. His head turns, once, twice. This is it—the end. For real this time. Or is it?

Davinder used to join me out on the field every once in a while, before shepherding the goats in for the night. Sometimes, he brought along sugar cane to chew on or roasted peanuts he grabbed from the kitchen. His favorite scenes were of Arthur and Franz's pretend shoot-outs.

Once, as Arthur theatrically clutched his chest, mouth wide open in a soundless scream, Davinder, too, threw himself down onto the dusty earth, legs twitching, shoulders rolling, spine writhing. Suddenly he stopped, and all I could hear was the soft murmur of the movie on my phone.

But then he got up, ready to get back to work. *Save this seat for me, will you?*

This is how I remember him now: the dark outline of his silhouette against a pale, hazy sunset, enveloped by the herd of goats, calm only around him and no one else.

PUNJABI APPAREL

We have to leave the van behind and cross the mountains by foot. The agents didn't tell us about this part beforehand—or had they? I never read the small print. By the way everyone is dressed, seems I'm not the only one.

The mountains are real, but we are dressed for our imaginations, a Punjabi version of that global all-American look. We are wearing jeans, striped shirts, and sneakers, Adidas tracksuits (mine is a knockoff I inherited from Davinder: *Abibas*), or big-sleeved poufy letterman jackets, striving to look like a postcard of Sylvester Stallone from the '80s our fathers had propped up at the half-blind mirror by the sink, behind a tin in which they stored the utensils to tend to their beards.

Harbir is the only one who's chosen sturdy boots, sensible worker's trousers with many pockets and a windbreaker.

We are walking up toward the great whitescape, the border of the world as we know it. Turns out, there is a difference between seeing the snowy mountains from afar—*a pretty picture! like a painting!*—and actually crossing them.

A bleak chill creeps up as we ascend, working toward my innards, finding its way into my bones in no time.

FROSTBITE

Gangrene formation means localized death (waxy and without pain).

NADEESH'S FEET

A frozen foot doesn't look the way I thought it would. I once saw an image of a man who got frostbite on his limbs while hiking in the Himalayas. Purple and black, they weren't identifiable as legs and feet anymore. Black-hole limbs, disappearing fast, bitten by an alien disease. Nadeesh's feet, on the other hand, have turned angry and red, growing pustules and bumps like an aggressive vegetable. But maybe they're still in the initial stage. His face contorts in pain when he pulls off his socks.

Amrit tries to carry him for a while, hoisting him over his shoulders like a goat carried to the slaughterhouse. But he keeps slipping and falling. Harbir, without saying a word, takes over. But, even for a warrior like him, it is impossible to carry a grown man through so much snow. He puts Nadeesh down.

The agents walk onward, half disappearing in fog.

EUROPE: ARE WE THERE YET?

"Are we there yet?

"Are we where yet?

"Are we at the point yet—the point in time where you tell me what's going to happen next?"

"I'm not going to tell you what's next, Happy."

"You're not?"

"No."

"No? OK."

"You must figure that one out for yourself."

"Ok. But—"

"But what?"

"I mean . . . since you basically brought me here, I thought you'd sort of . . . lead the way."

"You have brought yourself here, Happy. It is your accomplishment alone that you have come this far. And only you can figure out what is next. This is very important to remember."

"Well—I did not come entirely by myself, did I? The coordinators brought me here. They coordinated the trip. And you did nudge me in the direction of leaving. Remember how you were painting a picture—"

"Still, you made the decision. I just followed protocol."

"The protocol for what?"

"It's very important that we get this right. For legal reasons, as this is being recorded. You decided. You signed the contract."

"This is being recorded?"

"Well—I—yes. That's in the contract, too, right at the end . . ."

"I didn't read the small print. Come on. It was two in the morning. I was half-awake, half-dreaming. I just clicked 'Agree.' It was a bit of a hassle to photograph my signature on a piece of paper, then send the image and insert it, but then the contrast wasn't right, and I had to edit it, until—"

"We've been paperless for a while at the ministry. It's just the responsible thing to do."

"Just saying, you know what state I was in when I signed that thing! I was desperate. I couldn't sleep. I was stuck in a rut."

"Only you know what state you were in, Happy. You are the sole author of your destiny."

"Oh, right, as this is being recorded, is it? Who is it being recorded for?"

"For quality assurance, we reserve the right to record all conversations . . ."

"OK then, all right. But who keeps it? All these conversations? Who listens to all of this?"

"They keep the audio upstairs for a while and then it is transferred to Legal, just in case. And finally, after five years or so, it is stored in the Archive."

"The Archive? What archive? For how long?"

"The Archive where all things are stored in the end. I've never been. But I know it's there. I don't know for how long exactly. I guess—forever?"

LOG OF TRAVELERS: BARI

AMRIT SINGH PURI (*1991)

HAPPY SINGH SONI (*1991)

HARBIR SINGH BHARAJ (*1988)

~~NADEESH NIHANG~~ (*1990–2010)

SUKHA DHILLON (*1986)

~~VASDEV SINGH SARAI~~ (*1991–2010)

IN THE BEGINNING,
WE WERE SIX

When we get off the boat at Bari, there are only four of us.

ONE MINUTE OF SILENCE

Let's have a minute of silence. One minute of silence to remember what is lost. You are not to utter a word. OK—ek, do, tin! I am starting the count—now. You are to remain still, close your eyes, and breathe. Your thoughts are fast-flying clouds, spread across a creamy sky; the winds are strong today. Your thoughts cannot be held on to. They appear and disappear in quick succession. You do not pause to look at them. You simply let them go. As they appear, some clouds

are plush and jolly, some thick and stormy, others wispy and neu-
rotic; you own none of these clouds. They are part of the sky, you
see. The horizon owns them much more than you do. The crows are
their caretakers. They appear ill-tempered at times, but they mean
well. They are ancient, far older than you will ever be. Please, do
remain silent. I know you have the urge to speak. To speak even
before they finish their sentence. You think you know. What I think,
what I will say; you believe yourself to be omniscient of my arguments
and anecdotes. Consider this: you might not know anything at all.
Like your sense of smell, you had to let go of your old ego some time
ago. In the desert maybe, wound around a dead plant by the foot of
a dune—an ego like a smoky snake, taking on the form of a clever
crow, flying up into the sky, to find a carcass on which to feast.

Yes. A real minute can seem like an eternity. But you see—it is
over already. And now you may speak again.

PART
TWO
I AM A BAG

‥

CALL ME WHEN YOU GET THERE

AMBIKA: happy, are you ok?

FATEHPAL: hey—are you there yet?

FATEHPAL: can't reach you brother . . . get an Italian SIM!

AMBIKA: call me when you get there!

@JASSY_DEOL: how are you, gorgeous? greetings from dubai.

TRENITALIA FR 9560

The Italian interregional train is as close to flying as I've ever come. Racing up the side of the boot to meet its center, where all roads lead. Rome. I whisper the words *Pescara Centrale.* This is where I am going to change trains. My destination is Roma Termini. *Roma Termini.*

The lady on the opposite seat is glancing at me over her newspaper. I smile without showing my teeth. For now my goal is to blend in, not stand out. I try to cover the holes in my Abibas jacket with my hands. Discreetly, I sniff around my armpits. A hot shower is awaiting me in Rome for sure. Not just a shower, but a proper bath. Past the freshly painted picket fence and the German oak where the Dutch maidens are shitting cheese, in a snow-white house with a view magnifique waits a lustrous, luxurious bathroom made entirely of Makrana marble. Faucets of 24 karat gold spurt foamy, fragrant water into a deep basin. Above the tub, a crystal chandelier made of sugarcane jaggery—from which a flock of rose-ringed parakeets will be feasting joyously. Which is why this bird shit isn't your average toxic goo, but the finest liquid soap imaginable. Yes, this time it is the birds who are shitting, their soap raining down my body and into the water, to dissolve and froth and produce bubbles of extraordinary diameter and delight.

VOCABOLARIO

sono felice

I AM A BAG

I am a bag. A bag in a luggage storage facility in Rome by Termini station.

I am of medium build, made of cognac leather. I once was the skin of a cow, tall and brown, moody and broody, feeding on the juicy meadows of South Tyrol. Now I am a skin, a room, a container. I've traveled far and wide: Bulgaria, Uzbekistan, Mexico, the United Arab Emirates, Napoli, and Lucerne.

I would say I am built to be content. Not happy, but content. I believe in what is tangible. I am thick-skinned and pigheaded. I am strong and sturdy.

A pipe is leaking water onto my skin, infusing me with an uncomfortable case of mold. I have been waiting for a while. Days turned to months; months turned to years. I do wonder what happened to my owner. I miss his hands on my handle.

Instead, a brown man is resting his head on my shoulders. He arrived yesterday. Fresh off the boat. Water from the leaking pipe trickles along his neck into his sweater. His hair is greasy. I can smell that he has not encountered a warm shower in a while.

It is a truth universally acknowledged: that a human being needs a place to rest their head. Also, they need something to carry their essential items. Fortunately, I am both. So I will always be needed. I'm comforted by the thought.

The luggage storage, North Indian owned, is also a limbo for illicit arrivals from the homeland. Soon, these Indians will be born into their new European reality. For now, they are waiting in damp, dark corners. Time as you know it doesn't apply to a luggage storage facility. This space is a forever waiting room.

A ROOM WITH NO VIEW

A room mustn't necessarily be attached to a view. A room and a view could exist separately, quite happily, side by side.

When I lean against the windowpane of the storage facility, up above, I can see a small rectangle of blue sky.

SOFT SKILLS

Coordinators are not exactly headhunters—but they do take the trouble of job hunting off your plate. And completely out of your hands. I have provided a pdf of my CV, but I am not sure anyone has read it so far. Should I make it more accessible—short and sweet? I have read online that you should be able to summarize your core skills and goals in just one sentence. The coordinator's job-matching leaves something to be desired. Whenever they text me, I get the sense that they're not taking into consideration my considerable soft skills.

EU—DIRECTORY

The Department of Irregular Arrivals	E 0 U<I
The Department of Irrational Fear	E 1 B<Y
The Department of Brochures, Museums, Archives, Maps, and Confusion	E 8 N<Z
The Department of World Heritage, Border Control, and Insulation (including but not limited to felt, hay, historians, cellulose, fat, fences, walls, sanctions, and matters of the Mediterranean sea)	E 1 C<Y
The Department of Cheese and General Milk Products	E 2 L<Z
The Department of Darlings (you know who you are)	E 3 U<Z
The Department of Debt and Currency Exchange	E 3 U<V
The Department of Butter, Gouda, and Ricotta	E 1 K<Y

The Department of Imposter Syndrome and Delusions of Grandeur	E 1 M<XL
The Department of Guilt and Cabbage	E 2 N<Q
The Department of French Cinema, Stimulants, and Unions	E 5 K<Q
The Department of Rage, Repression, and Micro-Aggression	E 0 N<N
The Department of Transcontinental Affairs and Choses d'Amour	E 6 L<3
The Departments of Objects We'd Rather Like to Keep	E 7 K<Q
The Department of Parks and Recreation	E 7 K<Q
The Department of Monumental Shadows	E 0 U<0
The Department of Energy (nuclear and not), Climate Protection, and Affordable Housing	no room yet assigned

THE COORDINATORS

DEEP: have u worked in a restaurant before?

HAPPY: no

HAPPY: but u know what, I'm quite the foodie so I think I'm the perfect match. :)

DEEP: M will send u address tomorrow. 6 a.m. sharp. No open shoes, yeah?

FILETTI DI BACCALÀ A SANTA CECILIA

4.5 ★★★★★ 1,234 REVIEWS

€—ROMAN RESTAURANT

Fried fish, plus typical local salads and snacks in a basic trattoria with a lively terrace

ADDRESS: Via dell Monte Farina, 37, 00186 Roma, RM, Italy

SERVICE OPTIONS: Dine-in—Takeout

HOURS: Mon–Sat, 17.30–22.30 h

DON

Close to Campo de' Fiori, this place is known for its fried salt cod, as its sign—Filetti di Baccalà—suggests. The hours are inconsistent, but once there, walk straight to the back and order directly from the ladies frying the fillets. The batter might be a little too thick for my taste, but it's still a delightful evening snack. Eat with very cold beer.

SIMONE WORLD TRIATHLON CAGLIARI

The cod is moist, the batter is crispy and fragrant—what else could you ask for?

GLOBE OTTER

Italian waiters are ruuuude, man. We had to wait for ages 'til they took notice. Also: no pizza? What Italian restaurant doesn't serve pizza? Fish tasted like . . . nothing. They could, like, season the batter?! Beer was OK. Gf liked the beans. Two out of five stars.

FI LET

Fish like flower blooming on tongue. Not much decor—no fuss, no airs—I like it much.

VIOLA

Others have said it before—I will say it again and again: the best fried fish in Rome. Possibly the best fried fish I ever had. A hearty portion, light and crunchy and salted just perfectly. I will return again and again and again.

EUROPE: DO YOU

"Europe, do you have a minute?"

"Yes. Only a minute though. They pushed the next meeting forward, but I still have to go through my notes beforehand. And there is a troublesome case in the South of Italy. I think we will have to terminate the agreement soon."

"Oh dear. Well, I hope you can work it out. I was just wondering: before I arrive, do you have any last advice?"

"Just be yourself, Happy. Be empathic, flexible, and resilient. Do you."

"OK. So, you think just being myself will do the trick?"

"Yes. Absolutely. Though, now that I think about it, there might be just one tiny little thing. I am not sure how to put it . . ."

"Just say it. Don't spare my feelings. I need any advice I can get."

"You know, people might take you more seriously if you weren't always so . . . kind. So very smiley. Do you know what I mean? Coming across a bit more . . . serious would suggest strength. Drive. Leadership skills."

"OK. Yeah. I just assumed being kind was the general idea. I don't know . . . isn't this what people want? What makes them feel good? A big smile. Saying yes and please. Spreading harmony."

"Of course. I apologize if I confused you."

"You didn't confuse me. So . . . I shouldn't smile as much as I currently do."

"Yes. Although it is a splendid smile. Lovely white teeth. Work on your posture, too: Straighten your spine, stand upright. Look, here. Shoulder blades pulled back a little more. Lift your chin."

"Like this?"

"Yes! Excellent. Imagine . . . imagine, you could spread your wings and fly!"

"OK. Yes, I get it."

"Take up space. But not too much! Might cause trouble, step on people's toes. Find the balance. Maybe—no, you will be fine. Perfectly fine. OK, I really have to hurry now. Good luck!"

USEFUL PEOPLE

5.45 a.m., Rome, Via del Monte della Farina. The alleyways are vacant, except for the odd pedestrian working in the service industry, entering shops and restaurants through back doors. Eyes and limbs half-asleep, carrying the faint shadow of a night too short, such workers turn up no matter what—to be hospitable, to be of service, to take care of you. I am proud to be part of this early cohort of useful people.

I locate myself on my phone, blue dot hovering along faithfully. Almost there. Then I recognize the slim green door from a photo I saw online. My first role as a European is an exciting rite of passage: the Waiter/Aspiring Actor.

I go through the notes on my phone one last time. I jog in place and shake my arms, massage my jaw to release tension and do a few speech exercises (*a e i o u, a e i o u*). I square my shoulder blades and lift my chin.

I knock once, politely.

I knock once more, a little harder.

After a few seconds, I use my fist to bang against the wood.

Finally, an old Italian woman, well over sixty, opens the door and stares at me blankly.

"Buongiorno! Sono Felice."

Within a week, the scent of fried cod pervades everything I own: my hair, my fingers, even my underwear. By the end of a shift, I feel as if I myself have been covered in batter and fried multiple times, ready to be served.

A BRIEF HISTORY OF FRYING

Let us first, before anything else, talk about the sound. Close your eyes. Envision a pot filled with hot oil, in which you then carefully lower a pakora. Shy sizzling grows into a full-bodied crackling. A sound equally calming as raindrops on a tin roof all night long. The white murmur of cooking. This sound can heighten in volume and intensity. It can evolve into a full-on tropical rainstorm if you decide to add more pakoras.

The oil is now at a full boil, producing a foaming sea of so many bubbles that cannot ever be counted. The pakora is totally surrounded, every crack and crevice getting cooked to a crisp. You are surrounded, too: the sound and the smell enter every pore of your skin, enveloping your hair most lovingly, persistently. The pakora will turn brown and golden, as will the oil. Careful—if too many crumbs of the batter get lost in the pot, instead everything will blacken, turn bitter.

Frying is a highly immersive experience—a fast and furious game. To fry well, you must be of bold character; decisive with a strong will. Punjabis are well-known lovers of deep-fry. A great-aunt of mine fried away half her hand on the quest for perfect samosas.

The North Indian way of frying fish is quite extraordinary. Fresh fish is diced into chunks, dipped into runny chickpea batter, and deep-fried until perfectly bronzed and crispy. Ladle after ladle of pakoras land on sheets of newspaper, which turn oily in seconds. Sprinkled with masala and lime juice, served with onion rings and mint-coriander chutney, still blistering hot, they disappear into all kinds of mouths—pakoras do not discriminate.

Frying as a cooking technique was likely invented in an ancient Egyptian kitchen around 2500 BC. In India, Tamil people were deep-frying Vada as early as 100-300 CE, using leafy greens, gourds, and pulse; a delicacy prepared on festive occasions. Frying didn't become fashionable in Europe until much later, during the Middle Ages—but only for rich people. Animal fat was expensive. You couldn't use up a whole pot of lard if you were poor. The first recorded incident of frying in Europe has been traced back to a seventeenth-century painting that depicts an old lady frying an egg. It is called *Old Woman Frying Eggs*.

I zoom in. An old lady, and yes—two eggs frying in a small pan. She is about to crack open a third. There's a boy in the picture, too. He is probably a delivery boy, rushing in between merchants and taverns, always running late. Can't be older than fifteen. The frying lady reminds me of the resident fortune teller in our village. The bird-like look of her, the spaced-out gaze; an uncanny resemblance. Everyone turns to this woman for the central questions in life: *When will I marry? Will I live long? Will I give birth to a boy?* No one is upset when her predictions don't come true. She tells us exactly what we want to hear: a little lie, embellished beautifully.

JUST STAY PUT

To start with, I made a lot of mistakes. I massaged the fish lovingly. I began in the middle, near the spine, and moved my thumbs in circular movements over the aching white flesh of the cod. These big guys tend to store their tension in their lower backs, as most people do.

Since Bari, I haven't been able to tilt my head to the left—hurts like hell. A blocked nerve maybe.

You don't have to massage it! That's what you do to Kobe beef, not fish. Don't ever touch the fish again. Don't even go near them. Rosella, the head fryer, had pulled me away from my new fish friends toward the batter preparation station, and that's where I am to stay. In spite of my people skills, I am given no customer contact whatsoever, no chance to be seen, to be discovered—sometimes not uttering a word all day. I remain in the back of the kitchen, dashing between storage, fridge, and frying station, trying to guess what the others mean when they holler.

> *wait*
> *just stay put*
> *don't move*
> *it must have been*
> *a mistake*
> *they sent*
> *the wrong one*
> *didn't we ask for*
> *oh boy*
> *he needs to go work with the cows*

Punjabi, they go to Gran Padano. Cow experience. Milk people.
No fish people. No sea close by!
How will he know how to handle fish?
I don't know, why do you keep asking me?

The whole Filetti di Baccalà crew is proficient in Italian, in frying, and life in general: Rosella, the beating heart of the operation; the dishwashers, Bo and Champ; Rudy the line cook; Giuseppe the barman. I try to listen in, and learn, but I'm slow to pick up their threads of conversation. Thus, I sit at language's fraying edges, lulled into calm by the rise and fall of their intonation.

ROSELLA

Rosella is tall for an Italian lady, brimful of something sparkling and glorious. A crisscross of wrinkles plays around her eyes like the sea on a sunny day. I know what that looks like now, having seen the sea and crossed it, too. The occasional storm can be scary, but, even when seas swell, you can be sure that the sunlight will return once more. The nail on Rosella's right thumb is missing. In the beginning I was scared of her, as she is loud and teases everyone mercilessly. She runs the kitchen like she owns the place and, like an oven, emanates a nurturing and benevolent heat.

Rosella's late husband, Horace, a carpenter by trade, had been working on movie sets in Cinecittà until he died of pancreatic cancer nine years ago. His end wasn't peaceful and it wasn't painless. Whenever she's concentrating, you can see all of this accumulated in the lines on her forehead. The last gig Horace had worked was Martin Scorsese's *Gangs of New York*. None of it had actually been filmed in New York.

Rosella remembers walking through the set of Paradise Square in the immigrant enclave of Five Points, imagining the American city as it must have once been, with the sweet rotten smell of sewage and cries of war in the air. She had even promenaded on the deck of one of the two full-size ships in the New York harbor—all built by Horace and a small army of fellow carpenters, masons, bricklayers, and ironworkers. Horace, on his lunch break, had pointed out the different kinds of woods and his reasons for using them while she'd craned her neck trying to catch a glimpse of a passing star— Leonardo DiCaprio maybe? She never got to see anyone famous, at least no one she would have recognized, but she did have a little chat with the hair and makeup girl, who was responsible for curling the hair of Cameron Diaz each morning—and that was still something, wasn't it? As far as anecdotes go.

THE GULMOHAR SEED

A gulmohar seed pod is surprisingly large. Inside, the seeds are displayed in an orderly fashion, cooped up in their individual rooms. It's tight quarters in there, but at least they all have a bed of their own. Three months after my departure, Soni Square was torn down and reduced to amber dust—an empty plane, awaiting the arrival of Wonderland Annex I: Punjabi Waterworld. Before vacating the premises,

Gul had taken a seed pod from the old tree and saved it inside her sewing box.

Today, she is looking for that box in Ambika and Jiten's big house in Jalandhar.

The earth is hard and dry, but Gul's hands are strong, and she fills the pot with enough to bury the black seed. Before she pushes it in with her forefinger, she cuts it very gently with a kitchen knife—this wakes it from slumber. Even this small injury: an act of love. After she waters the earth, she will have to wait—and trust. Even the most beloved seeds, planted with the greatest of care, sometimes resist the urge to grow.

A MOONLIGHTER'S PAYROLL STATEMENT

WAGES
€20 per day

DEDUCTIONS
Income Tax:
zero
Health Insurance:
zero
Pension Plan:

zero
Benefits:
zero
Union fees:
zero
Room & board:
€241.00
/month
Loan repayment:
€11,987.10

comes out to, let me see, eventually,
magnanimously,

in the red
(forever).

LOCATE ME

Locate me
below
bars
underneath
tables
behind
stables
In the back of the

van
In the back of
my mind
In the back:
this is where you are.

BO AND CHAMP

Bogdan and Champo—Bo and Champ, for short—are the dishwashers of Filetti di Baccalà. Champ is a Tibetan cool kid whose floppy
black hair is greased back like Elvis and who wears fake Gucci sweat-
ers to work. Bo, originally from Poland, is wispy as a birch tree. His
watery blue eyes are perpetually staring into outer space, even when
he's talking directly to you. They both smoke a lot of weed before
and after work, which makes Bo quieter and Champ even more exu-
berant than he already is.

Inseparable, they even share a room above the restaurant. They
have been around for a while—and I like to be around them. They sing
to me in a register I know: Beavis and Butt-Head, Starsky and
Hutch, Salman and Madhuri. I can lay back and relax and just enjoy
the show.

CHAMP'S KAMA KAMA CHIARO DI LUNA SONG

Heeeeeeeeey, buongiorno tutti! Come stai?

Kama *means work in Nepali, OK? 'Cause work is what we*

gotta do, work is what we're here for . . .

Chiaro di luna! Chiaro di luna! Chiaro di luna!

Scrub-a-dub and grub and pan, man

Scrub-a-dub and swish, insane, man

Fry da fish and cash and carry

Hot and gold and kiss and crackle

Kama kama kama kama

Scrub-a-dub and grub and pan, man

Scrub-a-dub, and swish, insane, man

Boil the gold 'til it's all black and

fry da fish and cash and carry

Have a smoke—nooooo—heavy heavy

Kama kama, chiaro di luna!

Scrub and sip and nap—no never—

out the door and rollll, my fella

GTA, asleep, repeat, man

GTA, asleep, repeat, man

Repeaaaaaaat, man!

Kama kama kama kama—chiaro di luna! Accendi

da luce!

Irregolari, irregolari! Off-the-books Cinderellas forever

Give me that mullet any day, in fact, cut my hair

right now:

business in front, party in the back
This is the kama kama chiaro di luna back-of-the-
kitchen song,
by yours tru-lyyy lalala,
brrrrrrrrrrrrrrrr,
Chaaaaaaaamp

VOCABOLARIO

Questo è il pane di ieri?

Io faccio volentieri.

SIGHTSEEING

SANTA CECILIA IN TRASTEVERE

Recommended by Rosella (Santa Cecilia being the namesake of Filetti di Baccalà). This renowned basilica was built on top of what was once Cecilia's house. I can sympathize. It's like how Wonderland was built upon the remains of Soni Square. But I guess all houses stand on the foundations of those that came before.

Cecilia herself is resting here—her *relics*, which just means body parts? I imagine individual bones and bits of skin encased inside the fine marble sculpture of a woman swathed in translucent fabric; we cannot see her face, just a bit of her neck and her ears, with her delicate index finger pointing toward me—her hands look like they'd been tied up for a while and the rope has only just been unbound.

VATICAN MUSEUMS

The line for the Sistine Chapel goes up all the way up around the corner and then some, plus the entrance fee is €15. I decide to skip the Vatican Museums.

FONTANA DI TREVI

At the Fontana di Trevi, I lean over the banister and get out my phone to watch Sylvia, aka Anita Ekberg, in *La Dolce Vita* taking a bath here with the well-known paparazzo looking on.

Marcello, come here! she calls out to him, as she walks toward the water falling picturesquely from above. She looks sublime in her figure-hugging black dress, dreamy, zoned out. Not quite *sane*, but blissfully unaware of that fact. Later, following her, he says: *Yes, I guess, she's right. I'm making a mistake. I guess we're all making a mistake!* He traces her outline like an artist would trace the sketch of a perfect sculpture on a piece of paper. It is night, the fountain is beautifully lit, and there is no one else around . . .

Quite a stark contrast to the hustling scene of the present moment. It's so crowded, you have to fight for the best spots to take a picture; a group of teenagers is sitting down on the pavement with their McDonald's takeaway, squirting the brightly colored sauces onto their chicken wings, letting the empty packets glide onto the pavement. A crow is approaching, beak inclined, in joyful expectation of free fries. Two women are leaning into me trying to take a selfie.

"Hi, could you take a picture of us?"

I take quite a few, just to make sure there's one they'll like. I pick an angle from which they both look equally lovely, slightly elevated, with the statue of Neptune positioned right in the middle of their ginger heads. Sadly, the fountain is switched off today. Quel dommage—a missed opportunity for some atmosphere.

"Grazie!"

They scroll through the photos, happily.

"Do you want a picture, too?"

I hand my phone over and lean against the banister, gazing nonchalantly into the distance. It would be cool if I were wearing a suit right now, like Marcello Mastroianni. And something to hold in my hands: a cigarette, a glass of wine, a thick leather-bound book. The photo ends up not being too bad—except there's a blue blur where some kid is running through the picture, and Neptune has disappeared somewhere right behind my head.

COLOSSEUM

This is it, where it all went down: Bruce Lee versus Chuck Norris, the legendary showdown, arguably the most iconic fight in cinematic history. Underneath an archway of dark columns, with a baby cat looking on. I love when Bruce, having killed Chuck in combat, turns back around to cover his opponent's dead body—the hardened, noble look in his eyes.

I have a hard time finding the entrance to the Colosseum. It's rather confusing; lots of tourist groups following guides with big banners, and vendors trying to sell Americans and Germans bracelets from Mali, as well as miraculously whistling birds made from tin.

I will never forget when I first watched *The Way of the Dragon* with Davinder. The VHS was worn out from all the rewatching and rewinding, and the image was fuzzy at times, but it was so exciting I'd forgotten all about the spicy potato sticks in my palm and just stared at the screen, mouth wide open.

"Look at all these bad guys—too many! They keep coming. Bruce Lee can never beat them all."

On screen, Bruce Lee had come to the rescue of his relative in Rome—gangsters were presently trying to take over the restaurant.

"He'll knock them out. Every single one. Just watch!"

The scene went on and on and on.

"A long fight. It looks like they're dancing."

Davinder: his fist clenched, his shoulders swaying slightly, echoing Bruce's moves in his head. I leaned back against his knees and swayed with him, like we, too, were fighting, dancing.

"Happy, it takes time to fight all the bad guys in this world."

I AM A PIGMENT IN A PIETÀ

I am a pigment in an array of color between light orange and ochre, traveling back and forth eternally. I am part of a reddening, a blush, a pink light; watery and bright.

Milky understanding, yellow comprehending.

Particles of bitumen in varying proportions.

Rolling in the deep, beyond my light crust, lie secret layers of copper and brown.

I am hiding the muddy green of a pistachio thoroughly chewed. Painted with a brush so fine it could clean your dark long lashes.

I am a corner of an angel's mouth. The angel's skin is candy cotton soft. The glaze is divine. You might even be tempted to lick it. Come around. Come closer. You have to look at me properly. This is colore, darling. No disegno. No sharp lines.

An angel is holding a man's dead body, presenting it, ever so gently.

A second angel is bowing its head as though to kiss the dead man's head. Kissing and crying: these two activities are inevitably linked.

Those who kiss, cry.

The angels are here to help you mourn. Behold and pray. Take your compassion seriously. Also: never forget. Those you loved, and those who died.

Who assigned these angels their roles? Are they allowed to take a break once in a while? Do they ever lick the pistachio cream off each other's necks, very quickly, when no one is watching? Are they content in their perpetual mourning?

I have been wondering for centuries. But then, I am only a pigment, a glob of tempera grassa, oil emulsified with egg, on a faint memory of linseed oil, veiled with copper resin.

CASTING CALL: MALE LEAD, AGED 20–28

DESCRIPTION: Casting call for a film production to be shot on location in Rome and Tuscany.

LEAD ROLE: Male, aged 20–28, 5'9"–6', of athletic build.

Paid, Union and Non-union

Also seeking

EXTRAS: aged 18–55, local, must be proficient in Italian.

GENERAL STAFF & CREW: catering, set construction, runner, lighting, general assistance.

VOCABOLARIO

mal di stomaco
scintillante
opportunità
forse
tesoro

THE GURDWARA KITCHEN

I am singing to the rhythm of "Wahe Guru Sat Nam," like I learned to do as a kid from the Sikh women in the gurdwara kitchen—but only in my head of course. I am not entirely mad.

The cod is crispy, crispy is the co-ood, the cod is crispy, crispy is the co-ood. Roll around in crumbs, roll around in crumbs, roll around in crumbs. Crispy is the co—ooo—oood.

The women would sing as they kneaded and folded and rolled the dough into perfectly round rotis, never stopping, not even for even a sip of tea, keeping the rhythm beautifully. Their hands, too, were singing: a chorus, a choir, so pretty, quick, and graceful.

Gurdwara kitchens feed anyone who comes, anyone who needs a meal. I crave a simple palak paneer with a fragrant hot roti. Spinach cooked for hours with ginger and garlic, tender paneer cheese melting my tongue, filling my intestines. Lately, my body has been put on pause, but I think palak paneer is all I need to hit play.

ROOM WITH NO VIEW II

There is an upside to spatial limitations. Snug, tuck, prowess fast asleep; enclosed in tight quarters, like a dormant seed. A small room may provide necessary constraints. Push beyond the walls, and expand the field of imagination. Creativity and resilience will be honed and strengthened, without a doubt.

This time, my assigned accommodation is an actual room, in an apartment far out, close to the sea—at least according to the blinking blue dot on my map. I can't actually see the ocean from here.

I haven't met my roommates yet, as we all sleep in shifts, but they leave as proof of their existence an empty package of filter paper by the window sill, blue boxers on the bathroom floor, a dent in my mattress where another head used to be. I find a strand of blond hair and I imagine that it belongs to a guy named Igor, from Bulgaria. He is a line cook in one of those boozy osterias with the all-day happy hour specials. He doesn't talk much but makes an excellent ragu; so excellent indeed that it puts his Italian colleagues to shame. Thus, they try to make him feel small in little ways, giving him tasks below his station. But Igor doesn't mind. He is saving up money to open a tavern in his hometown of Veliko Tarnovo—he will call it the Lucky One and serve the best spaghetti al ragu in the whole world. Underneath the mattress, I find a crumpled-up piece of paper with recipes in a script I cannot read.

CINDERELLA-ELLA-ELLA, EH, EH, EH

My colleagues call me Cinderella. Something to do with being stationed by the oven and . . . being pretty? I am not entirely certain.

Whenever I enter the kitchen, they start singing "Cinderella" to the melody of Rihanna's "Umbrella."

Cinderella-ella-ella, eh, eh, eh . . .

Rihanna is a super famous world star, so it's a sure sign they have started to like me.

MONTANARA

Each morning before work, walking over from the train station under a slowly lifting sky of crows, plumage black and iridescent, sleepily looking for their first crumb, I proudly purchase a montanara from a corner-shop baker.

Best thing about montanaras: they are cheap. Second best thing: they are fried. Oh boy. They are fried all right. I have hardly tasted an equally fried thing in my life—and I am Punjabi. Imagine a fried roti-samosa-pizza-doughnut filled with tomato sauce. A Neapolitan specialty that takes on the form of a small mountain: a montanara. Perfect for any hungry human who is currently short on cash. The tomato and oil keep lingering in your mouth. Keeps you satisfied. Also, you've just swallowed a mountain. Makes you grow a few inches taller instantly.

VOCABOLARIO

Il mondo
possiamo aggiustarlo
melodia
non ho dimenticato

CAREER DREAMZ II

Bo is short for Bogdan, but Bo isn't short. Actually, Bo is the tall one in the family, and he is also the quiet one. In school, even when he knew the correct answer to his teachers' questions, he would take so much time rehearsing the exact wording in his head that the moment would pass, and so would the opportunity to speak—someone else had answered it already.

His shyness had also affected his love life. He'd been nursing a long-term crush on a girl a year above him. She didn't know his name yet, but he knew hers: Basma. Basma: fast-talking and unafraid, tender with her little siblings, long dark hair tied back so tightly her brows lifted slightly—eyes hungry, the color of acacia honey. Basma was planning to train as a nurse at the local hospital; he'd overheard her tell a friend while she was buying raspberry liquor, a generic Mars bar, and a lip pencil at the supermarket where he worked as a cashier after school. He'd looked down at the conveyor belt conveying away and mumbled, *Five forty-four, please, thank you, goodbye*.

Bo wanted to be like George Clooney in *ER* and save lives, but his grades were way below average. Plus, his father was a carpenter and no one in his family had ever gone to college, so becoming an actual doctor was out of the question. But maybe he could become a paramedic?

Yes, that would be his chance, his opportunity to shine. Basma would have to learn his name, wouldn't she, if he were the one to deliver the car crash victim to her, heroic in his bright orange uniform, with a brief, manly summary of the injury: *whiplash and spinal cord fracture. Trauma of third degree. No other survivors.*

She'd have to be like, *Thanks, Bogdan, that was expertly of you*, and smile at him over the stretcher. Then their fingers would accidently brush as she took the clipboard from his hands . . .

It took quite a bit of daydreaming till he actually googled "how to become a paramedic," only to learn that, since 2006, you needed a bachelor's degree. He left his thumb hovering over the sentence, then went back to restocking Coca-Cola bottles.

When Bo's elder brother asked him whether he'd want a job in Italy, Bo had thought for a moment, and then nodded, *Yes, OK*.

FATHEPAL: ON WORK

"Ok, Fatty, how many jobs is that now? Four? Five? I forget . . ."

"Stop calling me Fatty! Seriously . . . and, yeah, four. Ever since I had to close Masala Kitchen."

"Still sad about that."

"Yeah. My bank account is, too. It was just . . . the wrong location, I guess. The pakoras were excellent. Raju did a good job. No one wanted to eat them, though. People around here just order pizzas. Pizza Hawaii and Insalata Tonno, extra rolls, garlic butter, same same. Anyways . . . to what do I owe this honor?"

"How do you do it? Four? I am *dead* at the end of the day with just one . . ."

"Ha. Well. Restaurant *is* tough. Brother, what can I tell you . . . you get used to it. You get used to anything really. The work at the factory doesn't pay enough. Not enough to buy a house one day.

So when the gardening opportunity came up—of course, sure, happy to take it. I swear, they're *well-off* these people. He's a big *art* collector, you know. They have an actual Picasso—hanging in the wardrobe. Whole living room: white as snow. Everything in it either white or beige. Afraid to leave marks wherever I go. I take my shoes off, of course, but then I worry about smelly feet. I prefer the garden, the tulips, the hydrangeas, the chestnut, the acacia, the big oak tree. I keep the lawn so pristine, you could play hockey on it. I would *only* garden if I could, to be honest. But, when I asked for a raise . . . anyways. You just grit your teeth. Pull through. This is what you do. And, yeah, always have a goal in mind—a mantra. Like when you're playing Kabbaddi . . . *holiday, holiday, holiday, holiday. Chai, chai, chai, chai, chai. Big house with garden and central heating, big house with garden and central heating* . . ."

"Ha, OK. I see. Lots to learn still, I guess . . . oh, and, yeah . . . thanks again for that loan, Fatehpal. I really appreciate it. Only temporary. You will get it back. Promise. Once things pick up . . ."

"—Of course. Don't mention it. Family. No questions asked."

GLISTEN AND SHINE

Open on my phone is a film still of Sami Frey, wearing a trench coat and a black fedora. I'm wearing similar items that I found in a second-hand shop in Monti. Cost me a whole week of pay, but it's necessary to dress the part.

I slather a thick layer of Nivea on my face, rubbing the cream vigorously. If all else fails, glisten and shine. Hydration, hydration, hydration—a credo I've adopted from Babbu.

I look up the directions to the casting location once more. Easy. Know it by heart. Look again. Just once more for luck.

THE CASTING

"Ciao—posso aiutarti?"

"I'm here for the casting. The call for a male lead?"

"Ah, OK. Have you read the call?"

"Yes, many times. I have the newspaper clipping right here. See?"

"Yes, okeee, great . . . sorry, but that role has already been filled."

"It has? But it is . . . 9 a.m. Isn't this the first day of the casting? Sorry if I have misread . . ."

"No, no. It is. We just don't have any available roles for your typecast."

"Oh, OK. What is my typecast, just out of interest?"

"Well . . . male, eighteen to twenty-five—South Asian, I guess? You are Asian, right? Or Middle Eastern?"

"Indian. Yes. I see, OK. Any other roles that need filling? I am quite versatile, you see. Some even say I look like Sami Frey . . ."

"Sorry, who? You know, why don't you just leave your details and a link to a showreel, so we can get back to you should the need arise."

"A showreel. Yes. Sure. Where should I—?"

The woman points to a small blank space on her iPad, the cursor blinking expectantly.

I enter my name and my number. Then I just make up a link: www.happysinghsoni/unreal.com.

A BAR WITHOUT A ROOF

After closing, to cheer me up after my failed audition (*Not meant to be then, buddy!—they don't know what they're missing*), Bo and Champ take me to a bar called Tarantella Tropicale.

"A bar without a roof," they say.

A bar en plein air? Nice.

But when we arrive, I'm confused. The roof of the bar is intact. The ceiling is rather low, actually. It's a small and dingy place with sticky floors and a stage with three pedestaled poles illuminated in bright red, like spaceships in a low-budget film production.

I climb onto a bar stool and order a drink too sweet and syrupy to finish.

Suddenly "In Alto Mare" is blaring from two huge speakers. Then a woman climbs on stage and begins to dance. Swinging around the pole effortlessly, hoisting herself upside down and sliding along, as if her body is fluid, supple like water, or light. Like she is a hologram, Photoshopped onto a dark reality. Her hair is super short, so blond it is almost white. Her moves are rather experimental . . .

Oh. I see. A topless bar.

But as the dancer sheds her catsuit, it seems that atop her naked body she wears another layer of skin, pale and otherworldly. It's like she isn't really naked at all.

The song finishes. I applaud and smile and expect her to bow. It seems like the proper thing to do. But no one else is clapping.

At the bar after her performance, she asks for an ice water with lime and sits down next to me. Bo and Champ make googly eyes at me and give a thumbs-up.

"Hey."

"Hey. Hey, hey."

"I like your outfit a lot. Nice trench."

"Thanks so much! I like your catsuit, too, by the way."

"Oh, thanks! I make these myself, actually."

"What, really? That is amazing! Are you a Dancer/Fashion Designer?"

I like people who are many things at once. As a Waiter/Aspiring Actor, it gives me the feeling I'm not alone.

"Ha ha. No, no. I can sew, though. I learned it from my grandmother. I'm named after her."

"What's your name?"

"Luminita. But everyone around here calls me . . ."

She hesitates.

"What is it?"

"Marilyn Whirlwind."

"OK, cool. A stage name is always good. One for every personality."

"Exactly! What is yours?"

"Happy."

"Lovely. And your real name?"

"Oh . . . no. Happy is my real name."

"Ha. OK. Fabulous. Beacons of light and joy, aren't we? There must be hope for us still, with names like ours. Your name carries your fate. I know this to be true. Something my grandma used to say."

LUMINITA/MARILYN WHIRLWIND

Luminita means *little light*. It means little girl, long dark hair, wavy from braiding, eyes wide open, apple pie. From a village in Romania of less than five hundred inhabitants, she is named after her maternal grandmother. Luminita the elder carried a large tote bag everywhere she went. Nestled inside white cotton, lining yellowed over the years, you will find overripe apples, a Bible, and a spare headscarf, green and patterned with yellow ranunculus. She sold embroidered baby shoes to tourists by the main road and made black currant juice, thick and dark as Italian espresso. Then the first Luminita had died, and now Luminita means *alone*, the only Luminita left in the world.

Marilyn Whirlwind means rhinestone thong, hard-boiled and luminescent. It means black filter coffee, cigarettes, and walking home at dawn. It means lying down on a sofa with ears ringing from the bass, nose sore from the ingestion of finely milled substances. It means I put on a second layer of skin. A suit of armor, weightless and free. I had to leave Bucharest in a hurry, so I had to sew myself anew; once things go wrong they can go wrong again, believe me. Marilyn Whirlwind means I dance. It means I dance and you cannot touch me; I can't even touch myself.

EUROPE: DRESS-AS-YOUR-FAVORITE-CULTURE WEEK

On the train home, I lean my head against the window and stroke the milky glass with my fingers. Someone has engraved letters into the window with a knife. I can't read the words, but I can feel them. They speak of amore and revolution. The window and I are on intimate terms. It feels nice and cool. I lean my head against its tainted surface. I close my eyes.

I open my eyes.

A woman in a bright orange sari has entered the compartment. I have never seen an equally orange sari in my life. She looks unreal. A walking Fanta bottle. I suppress a giggle and cough. She turns around.

It's Europe.

"Europe!"

"Hello, Happy."

She smiles.

"I thought I'd try something new."

"I can see that."

"Do you like it? It's Dress-as-Your-Favorite-Culture Week at the Department of Arrivals."

"Well, it's certainly bright."

"You don't like it."

"Not every complexion can pull off orange; it's a challenging color. But the cut suits you perfectly. It is made for you."

"Is it inappropriate you think?"

"I'm sure it's fine. I mean it could be . . . No. Not at all. Rather brilliant I'd say."

"How are you today, Happy?"

"I am well, thank you very much. Tired. We went to a bar without a roof. Which included women taking off their catsuits plus sugary drinks. To be honest, I think I am a little bit drunk."

"Sounds . . . eventful. You don't need to tell me everything, Happy. Boundaries are a nice thing, too."

"Well, you asked. I had the feeling our relationship is quite . . . confidential."

"It's my job to make you feel that way, Happy. I am still your recruiter, though. But it's good to see you're adapting well to your new situation. I'm glad you are socializing. How do you find the frying business?"

"It's all right. Yeah. Fried food seems to attract good people. But of course, there is room for development, careerwise."

"There always is. That's the right attitude. And the European experience—is it all you imagined? More?"

"Oh, well, yes—it is . . . different. But, you know, after the journey . . . all good. I do appreciate the food."

"You do?"

"Yes, I love it. I mean, it's the best part."

"Would you say food is more important than work?"

"No work, no food. Right?"

"Right. Work is the basis for it all. I sent you the diagram, yes?"

"I think so . . . yes, yes. You did. When do you think I can move further up in the pyramid, though? From basic needs to special needs? You know how I love to plan ahead."

"Soon! No worries, I—Oh, this is my stop. Sorry, must run! Namasté, Happy."

Europe presses her hands together earnestly, closes her eyes, and bows.

AMBIKA: IBS

All grown and independent now, aren't you? Living la dolce vita? Need to get used to it, still. The fact that you're not just a thirty-minute drive away. Any news to report from the Eternal City? Had any amazing food lately? I sure could use a break over here—a pausa. Right? I've downloaded this app that teaches you a new word per day. Just so I can keep up. Once you become fluent. Anyways, I, for my part, cannot eat a thing right now. These spectacular cramps—they always happen the very moment I lay down to sleep. The second I let go . . . like ants crawling through my intestines. No, that's not quite right: it's more like someone has my stomach in a chokehold. And it's writhing, putting up a good fight. My stomach wouldn't just give up, no. I disappear into the bathroom, disturbing Jiten, who's a light sleeper, and I bite into the fresh towels, inhaling the white scent of detergent.

It's stress, I suppose. Parents moving in, living *on top* of the in-laws on the first floor—I mean, you know Jiten's parents, quiet . . . distant. They don't interfere with the energy of the room much. In fact, sometimes—I know I cannot expect constant praise. Still . . . a little *appreciation*—right? Is it too much to ask? A thank you—a smile?

Gul on the other hand: a room-spirit-at-large if there ever was one. Crows on the roof, Amanjot dreaming of barfi, ventilator turning at the ceiling, the street vendor selling elephant apples—*everyone* in a radius of 164 feet will pick up on Gul's current mood. They will *know.* She will make sure of that.

I am a professional minder of moods atm. I should have gone to school for that. University of Changeable Moods. Enroll me now. I'd graduate with honors. PhD on how to be flexible, adaptable, wriggle wriggle, highly talented in forgetting your own needs while feeling the needs of others just as acutely as if they were your own. You were always going on about soft skills right? Well, there you go.

Send some pics when you can! Have you had spaghetti vongole already? And those sweet little rolls . . . cannoli? Really wanna try one day.

VOCABOLARIO

sacco della spazzatura
questa forcetta è sporca
quale direzione per Cinecittà?

ON MY BREAK

An Italian lady and her lover are chain-smoking in the osteria next door, gossiping between courses, which the kitchen fires out in a quick succession: cut beef on rake and tomatoes, drizzled with lots of olive oil; fettuccine al ragu; roasted wild porcini. The woman, immaculately made up, with clean-cut short black hair framing expressive eyes, lips painted ox blood red, is talking loudly, with big gestures, while her lover gazes at her with a vacant expression.

Oh, to be as confident as the purple nail on her pinky finger. To be as sure of a place, a time, a meal, a feeling. One day, I, too, want to sit down in a proper restaurant and give an order like that. There is an art to it, I feel.

Their service is overseen by the fastest waiter south of the station: Matteo, though that is not his real name. Originating from a family of strong women in a small Indian village by the Nepalese border, he looks cosmopolitan, graceful, and efficient as he runs, floats, cleans, assigns, and apologizes. His Italian is perfect, fluent, confident. His competence makes everyone feel at ease.

Back at our humble Filetti di Baccalà, sitting at a tilting table on tiny plastic chairs, a German couple appears to be arguing. The woman clenches her jaw and studies the menu sullenly. Maybe she'd hoped to eat at the fancier place next door, but her boyfriend hadn't gotten the hint. Suddenly, she erupts into a stream of angry speech, uttered too fast for me to hold on to any of the syllables. (Not that I understand German anyway.) Now he is rolling his eyes, which, boy oh boy, is a big mistake. I've worked enough dinner shifts by now to recognize the international body language of messing up.

The truth is they are both just very hungry. They'll be happy as soon as the fish arrives, alongside green beans and cold beer. You just have to give their mouths something else to get busy with. Stop talking, just once in a while.

FRANZ AND ODILE
ARE HUNGRY

Franz and Odile are hungry. The thrill of the escape has worn them down, but they do not want to admit it. Each waits for the other to suggest doing something normal for once. Nothing Kafkaesque or existential, just . . . simple. Couple-y stuff. Are they even a couple? Officially. This is another question that remains to be answered.

Odile suggests that they go out for dinner. They pick a cozy-looking place with checkered tablecloth and dim lighting. We won't disclose the location in case they are still being followed. Suffice to say, the tables are wooden, the windows are misty, it is warm, and there are big red pots filled with ragu that have been simmering for hours. The place is filled with couples, whispering over vegetables in beds of warm sauce, fingertips touching, entwining, laughing quietly over jokes only they would find funny.

SPAGHETTI VONGOLE

Where do venus mussels live? What is their natural habitat? Do they feel? Do they think? If they do, what is on their mind? Do they pair up in couples? Are they polyamorous creatures?

VOCABOLARIO

malinconia

dove stai andando

sforzi

bisogno di più olio

FAMILY MEAL: CHISCIÖL

Our line cook, Rudy, is originally from Tirana, in the Valle region, close to the Swiss border. Most days, he's responsible for staff dinner. While cleaning up, I watch him make today's family meal, a kind of thick roti, made of runnier dough and fried in oil, using buckwheat and wheat flour, soda, oil, salt, cheese—*you normally use Valtellina casera, but I couldn't find it*—as well as a large swish of beer and a bit of Rosella's favorite grappa. He tells me the dish's name: chisciöl. Quite a tongue twister.

He fries the dough until very crisp and serves them with finely chopped chicory and a bit of oil and vinegar. Only the lucky ones get them while they're still warm. Rudy sneaks me a small plate before anyone else gets to eat. The cheese is still runny. Could he possibly have a crush on me?

HORACE'S BLACK TURTLENECK

I am wearing brand-new clothes. Well: old new clothes. To be precise: Horace's immaculately preserved 1970s wardrobe. Rosella has gifted me a garbage bag full, smelling of mothballs and sandalwood eau de cologne. In a twist of fate, it appears Horace had the same build as me: tall, lanky, with only the slightest of paunches, after a particularly big meal.

I had been saving them for our son—but Ernesto, well, he never cared much for these. Never got around to donating them either. Do you want them? You seem to like this, what do they call it . . . vintage style.

I had replied that yes, I love the vintage style. I disappeared into the bathroom and changed into Horace's black cashmere turtleneck and cream slacks, paired with artisanal leather shoes in bright red.

Not fit for a kitchen, said Rosella, but never mind.

I clean away stacks of oil-stained plates from the service hatch, trying to catch a glimpse of the front of the house. There's only one table seated: four men and one woman in the booth at the far right. They're loud, taking up a lot of space, so that the whole place seems full. One man wears a pale green scarf—fabric thin and iridescent—and a tight shirt patterned in brown and cream. He is heavyset and tan in that way that Europeans seem to adore. Back home, were he to walk into a beauty parlor, they'd ask him whether they should remove the tan with a special chemical peel, make him fair and lovely. I notice that the diners are out of wine, their glasses all empty.

Rosella and Rudy are both outside smoking—no service in sight.

Here's my chance, I think. Seize the moment. Put your soft skills to use. You only live once. Or, well, maybe several times, but that is neither here nor there—

I take off my dirty apron, pick up a bottle of our house white, and walk right up to their booth. I stand in front of it, with that star-quality look of melancholy on my face, until they notice me.

The green-scarf man raises his eyes from his phone and glances at me over the rim of his slim reading glasses.

"I like your sweater. Suits you."

"Grazie . . ."

My ears feel warm. I can't think of anything else to say, so I turn to leave.

"Hey, leave the bottle."

He takes the wine without looking at me again, and, as I walk away, I imagine him rolling his eyes, laughing, his tummy vibrating through his expensive shirt.

MEND

Babbu tries to mend the clutter that has accumulated up on the roof terrace of Ambika's house—bit by bit, at a leisurely pace: a broken Bluestar AC, a few terracotta planters, a set of small plastic swings for Amanjot, and a speedbike that Jiten had given up on rather speedily. Whenever Ambika wants to throw something away (yesterday it was a burnt but otherwise perfectly fine frying pan), he tells her: *No. Give, give.*

It's raining a bit, but still OK. Not enough to go inside. Also, what would he do down there? Nothing. He'd just be in the way. Thus, he persists, and presses a broken shard down onto the open wound of a planter, waiting for the Loctite Super Glue to dry. It's got a precision nozzle to reach difficult areas. Babbu likes glue, adhesives generally. While he is repairing, he gets acquainted with the crows of the neighborhood. He's made contact already, with the help of yesterday's roti crumbs. His little acts of friendship (bribes!). He hasn't named these city crows yet. Naming crows takes time. Crows remember faces, you know. They remember which ones feed them and which ones throw rocks. They hide stuff (peanuts, crumbs, shiny bottle caps to use for their nests) and remember where they put it. They have burial rites, like humans. Crows recognize themselves in the mirror, like dolphins and chimpanzees. Babbu insists the crows have never targeted the Soni cabbages, stolen neither seeds nor seedlings. I think it may be the case that cabbages don't entice the crows as much as rotis do.

What does Babbu see, as he stares down into the neighbor's garden—can it be? A Persian leopard? A rather small one, sleek and unmoving. Waiting for his prey. A leopard is said to have descended the hills of Himachal Pradesh once, getting lost in the maze of Jalandhar's residential quarters, almost killing a man or two. Babu gets to his feet. No, of course not. What he's seeing is made of porcelain. Not an animal, only decoration. His eyes are getting worse. He needs a new prescription but he doesn't want to ask Ambika to drive him to the optician. She's got enough on her plate as it is.

Babbu has not encountered even a sixteenth of the Crows of the World. There's the Rook, Pied crow, Bismarck crow, Somali crow,

Mariana crow, Piping crow, Thick-billed raven, Bougainvillea crow, Cuban crow, American crow, Slender-billed crow, Western Jackdaw, Palm crow, Chihuahuan raven (is it teeny tiny, like the dog of the same name?), Fish crow, Jamaican crow, Australian raven, and the elusive beauty that is the Hawaiian crow—almost extinct now, having been displaced by human settlers.

Young crows live with their parents for up to five years, if they do not find a partner—the origin of their famous intelligence may lie in their protracted childhood, the sweet time they take to learn. Crows use traffic lights to crack tough nuts, placing them on the street at a red light and picking up the nut shards after the cars have crossed at green. They memorize, think ahead, imitate, speak dialects, better than some humans do.

Rain is dripping down Babbu's collar. Its intensity has increased: the drops per square foot and diameter per individual drop as well. It would be stupid to get all wet. Maybe he should go down after all. Is the glue dry yet? He moves his thumb tentatively—it sticks. The planter—as good as new.

THE HOUSE OF
THE RISING SUN

After the restaurant has closed, and all steel surfaces of the kitchen are scrubbed until they gleam, the crew is sitting and standing outside the backdoor.

Champ plays old film soundtracks from a portable speaker. "The House of the Rising Sun" comes on. Oh, I know this one. From *Casino*—I love that movie.

I start moving my shoulders, slowly.

I haven't danced in ages.

I wiggle my toes tentatively. And then I get up. An overpowering vibrating motion pulses through my body. It exits me through my fingertips and shines onto my audience, like a laser beam. I combine old Bollywood moves with a freedom of expression that you could only call modern dance. I even channel *Bande à part*: tap tap, light light, feet feet, snap snap.

Giuseppe raises his eyebrows and bursts out laughing. He calls Rosella to come and watch.

When "Gimme Shelter" by the Stones plays next, I switch to my Mick Jagger move, long legs and pulling-up knees. The lips are important as well; mouth very large, awfully hard to imitate.

That does it. The crew of Filetti di Baccalà breaks into cheering, whooping applause. Rosella calls out to me: "Hey there, good-looking!" Still in Mick Jagger mode, I blow her a kiss. Then I do my Punjabi moonwalk.

I am bringing the house down. Finally, the crowd loves me.

VOCABOLARIO

spugna per la pulizia

sei carina

quanto costa il treno per Parigi?

A ROOM WITH NO VIEW III

My new address is only walking distance to the Pantheon, in the back-yard of a bustling restaurant, beneath a crisscross of white laundry slicing the sky. The door to the storage room is dark green and heavy. It falls shut with a sound that implies a vault of great depth; there is a finality to it.

I find a purple sleeping bag, but it is too hot, so I strip down to my boxers and just lie on top of it. I stretch my toes until they touch the cool stone wall—the ego needs limits. I understand. As usual, my room is trying to teach me a lesson. I can hear pipes gurgling. Someone is having a shower.

This time, there's no trace of prior inhabitants, just metal shelves stocking rows and rows of pizza boxes. Hundreds of the same jolly Italian cook, presenting his perfect, moist, hot margherita, bespread with San Marzano tomatoes and fior di latte. I close my eyes so I don't have to see his smile anymore.

HOW TO FOLD A PIZZA BOX

Flap, flap, flap, fold, flap, close, find the latch for the hole
flap, flap, flap, fold, flap, close, find the latch for the hole
flap, flap, flap, fold, flap, close, find the latch for the hole
flap, flap, flap, fold, flap, close, find the latch for the hole
flap, flap, flap, fold, flap, close, find the latch for the hole
find the latch for the hole
find the latch for the hole
find the latch
hole
close.

CROWN OF CREAM

Behind the glass, rows and rows of candied orange and lime jellies, perfectly aligned with limoncello and mandarinello pralines, bountiful cannoli of the giant kind, sprinkled with grated pistachios, and glistening cassatine in luminescent green, carrying a glorious crown of cream and a single maraschino cherry each.

I could shrink until I became the size of a cherry and dive in headfirst. I would live inside the dolce and feast on the ricotta cream. The cherry would be my forever-rising sun. I could gaze at it from the dome of my land, which would be your land, too, if you wanted it to be. The red shimmer would warm my intestines and I could feed on her light. I would take off my clothes and extend my hands. Pistachio showers would cover me entirely. I would build a house from the fallen crumbs.

RHYME/REASON

The jobs assigned by the coordinators follow neither rhyme nor reason. After four months at Filetti di Baccalà, I am suddenly whisked away. Just when I'd finally made some friends and was right at the brink of local fame.

DEATH TO
THE RADISH

ö

I AM RADISH

My skin is red and taut. I am positively glowing. Not a mark on me. I am immaculate; made to fit your mouth and your perfect teeth.

My flesh is white. A consistency hard and crisp, yet moist.

I am one-dimensional. Inside me, there are no layers, just thin skin and crisp flesh.

I don't feel much. I am comfortably numb. I am made to be bitten. A crunchy sound: a crackle, a crisp, my crust, the sound of my skin breaking. I will be gone once I reach your molars: white, pink mush, a tongue, a twirl, down down down.

I am not perfectly round, tbh. A tiny tail is attached to my bottom. I used to be ashamed of it. Now I regard it as a testament of my growth.

I am the lucid light-pink red you didn't know was missing.

A pungent full stop to the sentence that is a dish.

Adornment to a bowl of greens, a sandwich, or a glazed Peking duck; cut open like a blossom, splayed out most invitingly.

I am radish. Eat me now.

I am 95 percent water, 3 percent carbohydrates, 1 percent protein. Just like a cucumber. In a minute, I might just forget who I am and turn into a fat little cucumber instead. My cognitive capabilities are not fully developed.

I am meant to be eaten.

Quitting is not an option.

Quitting means rejection; it equals certain death. To be sentenced to rot, to lose color and contour, before anyone has had a chance to taste me. Thus, I persist. I work hard toward eliminating all faults. There is only one model to follow. The path is clear.

Better hurry. This carton is becoming uncomfortable. We come in beautiful bundles, paired up, rubbing against each other, skin to skin: great expectations. But I am bored of the other radishes in my company: we all look the same and feel the same, thinking analog thoughts all day. We are not made for animated conversation. I feel I am losing my flavor.

I am moist and crisp, but only for the duration of this song. I hate the melody, tbh, the workers play it every day on repeat.

Pick me now. Pick me good. Pick me, pick me, just like you should.

RAVANELLO EUROPE LIMITED

Ravanello Europe Limited, located close to Latina, in the Lazio region of central Italy, is Europe's largest year-round radish farm. It is a futuristic sight: utopian—or maybe the opposite, depending on your disposition. A modern farm with its huge high-tech greenhouses, windowless storage facilities, and endless rows of foil tunnels, spanning over a hundred hectares of land, Ravenello produces millions of radishes annually.

At Ravanello Europe Limited, radishes are sown and harvested six days a week, fifty-two weeks a year. For quality assurance, both hand and machine harvesting are employed to extract both bunched and loose radishes from the soil. The products are then washed and packaged in a well-controlled environment, so your satisfaction is guaranteed!

Hand harvesting: that's where we come in. We are the *quality assurance*. I don't have a name tag, but if I did, it would read *Happy Singh Soni, General Farm Worker & Quality Control Associate*. The General Farm Workers are all Sikhs, and there's ten of us; more during harvest. We work exclusively in the smaller growing tents and in the fields en plein air. The large greenhouses are sown and harvested by state-of-the-art machines, which we hardly ever see, but we hear their rumbling from afar: giants from another time, a foreign country.

THE CONTAINER

The interior of my new home is the color of congealed blood. Like the blood I used to watch collect in hot puddles on the concrete floors behind the shed in Soni Square, whenever it was time to slaughter a Beetal goat. Beetal goats with those long hanging ears that frame their stubborn little faces, resistance in their eyes even while facing death. I'd named each goat, long before they were led away to slaughter: Amir, Mumpitz, Lalla, Lucky, Grumpy, and Beans.

Blood-red isn't a color I personally would have chosen. I would have preferred a supernatural sky blue, or a calming beer-bottle green. But then again, I have to work with what I got. And what I got is one-third of a shipping container.

Ravanello Europe Limited provides temporary housing for all its workers, a small village of shipping containers nestled behind a wildly overgrown apple orchard. I live in Ocean Network Express (ONE)—slightly bigger than No. 2 (COSCO) and No. 3 (Yang Ming Marine Transport Corp). Inside the container are metal bunk beds; outside, on our spacious "terrace," there's also a camping cooker, a garden hose, and a bucket—but that's about it for amenities. Instead of a door, we have a curtain made of green foil, lending the room an underwater gloom. I, for one, am just happy to have my own bed.

GUL: VOICE MAIL

Happy, whereabouts are you right now?

I cannot keep track. You keep changing your location. Better stay in one place. You need to stay in one place to build a life. Be patient, Happy. Good things will happen soon. If things are hard now, the good things are bound to arrive next. I heard it in your voice last time. I know you are not telling us everything. No need to spare our feelings. Your father is sensitive of course, but I am made of sturdy stuff.

PARADISE SQUARE

We, the General Farm Workers, are not the only foreigners at Ravanello Europe Limited. We are, however, the most pigmented—the
ones who've traveled the farthest to get here.

Our foreworker is Ukrainian, but we hardly ever see him. He only
drops by to inform us of new rules or upcoming changes in schedule.

The storage facility management and final quality control is done
by the Moldavians—they're quite jolly, always turning the radio up
loud, and always up for a bit of small talk. I don't know whether this
is a national trait or just coincidence. But then again, we only see
them at the end of our shift, when everyone's happy to be done for
the day.

Romanians wash and sort the bunched radishes into boxes and
preprinted packaging. Romanian women—I guess men's hands are
not tender nor diligent enough for the task? But these ladies work in
the big greenhouses, and we almost never meet. I just see them
arrive at dawn, some walking, some on scooters, some very young,
some elderly. Luminita I and Luminita II.

Most of the lorry drivers are Polish, as are many of the suppliers.

These Eastern Europeans don't live on the farm. So we don't
really get a chance to mingle. Everyone pretty much keeps to themselves. My Italian was actually progressing quite nicely—too bad it
isn't necessary anymore.

Most of the General Workers living in the containers are from
hometowns barely 30 miles from Jalandhar. We speak a familiar mix-
ture of English and Punjabi.

Our own little immigrant enclave; I christen the village *Para-dise Square.*

RESIDENTS OF CONTAINER OCEAN NETWORK EXPRESS (ONE)

HAPPY: A Room with No View IV

HARBIR: We gotta stop meeting like this. The world *is* small, isn't it?

ZHIVAGO: I don't think he's Sikh, actually. Moroccan? I overheard Harbir say something. Wears green dungarees. Was making bread when I first arrived. Nice smile.

ANTS: All the containers are populated by ants. Minuscule and black, hardly larger than particles of dust, they flock in herds and love, above all things, overripe bananas and sweaty legs. The ants crawl into the cracks and crevices of bedding, just as they seek out the folds of your skin for shelter. Their bites are barely noticeable but result in a lingering feeling of itchiness, like a dark thought repressed, or a dream deferred.

HARBIR, AGAIN

The corners of his eyes lifted only slightly when he saw me. The corners of his mouth inched just a tiny bit higher. But I knew he was happy to see me. How strange to part ways, and then meet again. Harbir has, in fact, been working here ever since we first arrived in Bari. Initially, the coordinators meant to send him to a leather factory, but Ravanello Europe Limited had needed additional hands for the season. It's a bit of a shock how much I've missed seeing a face from home.

In his own taciturn Harbir way, he tries to help me adjust, showing me the ways of the radish, introducing me to the peculiarities of vegetable work and to fellow farmhands. He seems different from when I first encountered him by the side of the road, next to Rama Electricals in Jalandhar, all those miles ago, before we'd begun our journey across continents. Somehow, he's gotten shorter.

Whenever I try to make casual conversation with Harbir, he doesn't seem very interested. He's always looking at his phone, texting (very slowly). I keep waiting for him to pick up the thread of conversation, but he sticks the buds into his ears and puts on Phil Collins. He thinks his taste in music is a secret, but Zhiv and I can hear it; they aren't exactly quality headphones.

On the wall next to his bed, I notice a photo of a girl wearing a pale green dupatta, holding a branch of bougainvillea and smiling into the camera.

ONE MINUTE ON THE FIELDS

I pause, stretch my back, droplets of sweat dripping down my spine, watching my colleagues in the rows in front of me: Tarsem carries ten boxes at once, stacked up high, all the way over to the trailer, where Harbir does the heavy lifting. Zhiv is kneeling in his green dungarees next to me, biting his lips in concentration, bunching radishes up at the speed of light and fixing each bundle with the multicolored rubber bands we all wear around our wrists. I'm still learning—pulling the bulbs, holding on to the leaves, forceful yet gentle, shaking off dirt, bunching most expertly.

It's almost 5 p.m. but the air is still sizzling. We're wearing T-shirts or scarves wrapped around our heads to protect us from Helios shining mercilessly down upon Latina today. Except for Harbir, who's always wearing his turban.

I'm hungry. I look at the bunch of radishes in my hands. Bit dirty, but all right. Nice and bulbous. That perfect reddish pink. I pick one, rub it clean on my shirt, and bite right in. Satisfyingly crunchy—I like that. Your teeth got something to do. A hint of sharpness, but not lingering for long. Watery. Water is good, though. I'm really thirsty.

We harvest cherry radishes: the pretty prom queens, lacking the substance of their bespectacled friends, the earthy-flavored magenta radish. The cherries sure look good in the supermarket aisles, though.

GURU NANAK

His skin is marzipan-like, his cheeks glazed in strawberry blush. Looking out at me through hooded brown eyes, generous pink palms raised in blessing, he does give a sense of calm and magnitude to it all.

I'd been carrying the framed portrait of Guru Nanak Ji with me this whole time, wrapped in a small red cloth Gul had given me to keep it safe. The cloth still smells of incense, rice, and ghee. It's been a while since I last prayed . . . I actually can't remember. But, right now, I could use a bit of company. I decide to position the picture as high on the wall as I can reach, so that Guru Nanak has a good view into the container.

We have to rise at 6 a.m. each morning, but I start getting up even earlier to pray. Soon, the prayers turn to more personal inquiries and anecdotes. These sunrise dialogues between Guru Nanak and me have become quite intimate. I tell him a lot of things I haven't talked to anyone about in a while.

> **HAPPY:** So, yeah, things have been good. Could be a *little* better, sure, but then, that's always the case . . . it just makes you stronger, right? How've you been, anyways?
>
> **GURU NANAK:** The world is a drama, staged in a dream.
>
> **HAPPY:** True that, yeah, I agree with you there. I do wonder, sometimes, when I'm very tired at night—back aching, knees hurting, feet destroyed—whether it was all worth it, you know?

GURU NANAK: Dwell in peace in the home of your own being, and the Messenger of Death will not be able to touch you.

HAPPY: OK, I guess—you mean, I have to make a home inside myself, right? Do you think, one fine day, I will have a house of my own though?

GURU NANAK: Even kings and emperors with heaps of wealth and vast dominion cannot compare with an ant filled with the love of God.

HAPPY: All right, no to worldly possessions then, I see . . . plenty of ants around, matter of fact. No, I never kill them. Not my style. Even out in the fields . . . I know, we do use poison to kill the vermin. Or what one might call vermin. I know there is no vermin. Every being deserves to live, right. I do take great care with the fledgling radishes, though. They are quite delicate, you see . . . need protection.

GURU NANAK: Whatever kind of seed is sown in a field, prepared in due season, a plant of that same kind, marked with the peculiar qualities of the seed, springs up in it.

HAPPY: Wholeheartedly agree. Though I am scared some-times, that I'll just end up here, living in a container forever . . . that I'll never be an actor. I'm losing track of my dreams . . . I've stopped writing. And I keep having these weird nightmares . . .

GURU NANAK: Owing to ignorance of the rope, the rope appears to be a snake.

HAPPY: Hm, yeah, you're right. I'm just in a weird mood, probably. I need candor and clarity. Looking ahead, I guess. But, tbh, I can't help looking back sometimes, when

I lie awake at night. Especially about Kiran—is it OK for us to talk about this? I'm not sure whether I—but, yeah, I really liked him. I did. I imagined it a thousand times. And he was dead way before his time—seventeen! That's too young, isn't it? Wouldn't you say that's too young?'

GURUK NANAK: Those who have loved are those that have found God.

HAPPY: That's nice of you to say. Though I'm not really sure—about the finding God thing. But I have found you, haven't I. Miracles can happen. In the most unlikely places.

GURU NANAK: Sing the songs of joy.

HAPPY: Well, I wouldn't go *that* far . . .

I could always count on Guru Nanak Ji to listen. And to be honest, he turned out to be far less judgmental than I'd assumed all my life.

THE LOVERS

One evening as we return from the growing tents, I find the frame lying on the floor, the glass shattered. We had only just become friends, Guru Nanak Ji and I. Who would try to sabotage our relationship, just as it was beginning to blossom?

As I kneel to pick Guru Nanak up off the floor, a small piece of paper falls into my hands. It's a painting, in miniature: Two lovers are riding on a huge white fish with sleepy eyes, amidst a deep lapis lazuli sea. The woman has a lioness's paws and tail, the man's torso is that of an elephant. Yellow marigold petals are strewn around them, bobbing up and down in the waves. An octopus with a human face hovers at the upper right corner, looking menacing.

The lovers are both dressed in a white so bright, they seem to merge into one.

I look closer. It's Babbu and Gul! Young Babbu and Gul. Younger than I am today. The resemblance is uncanny. I look at the tiny signature at the bottom: Babbu Singh Soni. I never knew my father was a Farmer/Artist. Nor could I have imagined the greatness of my parents' love, magnificent and mythical; as yet unscathed, the hope of a whole life ahead.

Now, it is the last thing I see before I fall asleep, and the first thing I look at when I wake up. The fish salutes me from the Other Side. The octopus remains at a distance. He will never catch the lovers; their light is simply too bright, and he prefers the darkness.

ZHIVAGO

Zhivago has *a generous face*. I didn't even know what that phrase meant until I met Zhivago. That wide smile, those chubby cheeks— facial features have been generously bestowed upon him. I don't know. Sometimes it's hard to describe something when you're up close. His eye color, for instance: brown with a hint of green.

Out of solidarity he likes to partake in our traditions, celebrating Vaisakhi harvest festival and even making bracelets for those who don't receive any red and gold threads from their sisters for Rakhi.

He's our head chef, the one to speak up; a creator, a born leader, a reflector and a generator, a percolator of great ideas. The air is different around him: fizzy, light, inspired. Also, he can bake. I mean he can really bake. Even without a proper oven, he manages to produce the fluffiest, milkiest buns you ever tasted, by using hot stones in a fire. He conjures stuff up from scratch. Can always make something out of nothing.

I AM FLOUR

I am a bag of wholemeal flour in an Italian supermarket. I'm a multitude container. Neatly packaged, smoothed over sadness for consistencies lost.

I almost forgot I once was a grain. Now, it seems I am destined to become dough, in the experienced hands of an irregolari at a radish farm. A whole supermarket of alluring options but he bought nothing else, just me. He's walking fast, holding me tightly—as he takes me home, I notice his legs are strong.

Back at his place, he opens me gently. I hope he washes his hands before he touches me. Never mind, here we go. Hands, filthy as they are, digging right into my soft core. And then comes the water. Unfiltered. Cold! I retreat and crumble. Oh boy. First time. What is it they say? Give in to your destiny. Just relax and let go. I am doing my breathing exercises, and this helps me to trust the process. In his hands, I am dough, becoming soft and smooth.

He scratches his eyebrows, leaving a white residue in between his eyes (slightly cross-eyed, for that matter; it's charming).

He works me like a pro. He uses his fists. His palms. His fingertips. Once you give in to it, the kneading is like a meditative massage. His hands are quite gentle for a laborer, I must confess. He looks happy, too. Serene, at peace. Soft tabla music is playing from a mobile phone to set the mood. He lets me rest for a bit, covers me with a dish towel. Time to dream of my future.

The thing is: Us flours, we want to be eaten. To be consumed. I wouldn't say it's a death wish.* An erotic sentiment more like. It comes from a lustful place.

I have rested enough. He notices I am nice and plump and smooth; the gluten has relaxed. The tip of his finger bounces off my newly formed skin. He splits me up and rolls me into eight round balls. I am not one, I am many. Lol. OK, then. Let's get it on.

I can feel the heat of the fire. I am aroused. I have literally warmed up to this guy. I am ready. I am dough, watch me grow. He throws me in, and the burning sensation begins.

*TO BE CONSUMED

The desire to be eaten is a strange part of our collective conscious-ness. We try to suppress it as much as we can. Stay present in the moment. Therefore, many myths about the afterlife surround our inevitable consumption.

For example: once you pass the digestive tract, a field of light surrounds you, and you are reborn as a seedling, snugly contained by the earth, like a warm fist holding a delicate object.

Or: on the human tongue, you transform into pure energy, fueling your consumer's body. In our age-old illustrations, this energy is symbolized by intricate lightning-like rays. These rays are the reason for all life on earth.

But no one wants to talk about the reality: gluten-intolerance-induced winds and malodorous toilet bowls, the noxious tunnels of canalization, the myriad consistencies of shit—oh dear. I shouldn't have even gone there.

STORAGE FACILITY

Twenty brown hands' worth of radishes. Two hectares of cabbage heads, carrots, unripe bananas, guavas, eggplants, ladyfingers, turmeric, honey, bone, fat, marrow, legs, heads, hooves, and blood.

Tires in all shapes and sizes, smelling of rubber and tar.

Dead goats (a raging pandemic, nothing to be done).

Dichlorodiphenyltrichloroethane (DDT), forbidden in some countries, widely available in India. Mixed into flour to keep the ants away.

Kush from Afghanistan, perfume knockoffs from Ahmedabad, ultraviolet umbrellas from Guangzhou, LED fairy lights from Malaysia, mobile phones from Taiwan, all the summer 2010 Zara dresses that didn't make the cut, bunched up and condensed into a textile cube, roughly the size of a female Indian elephant.

Secrets, meanwhile, tend to be stored in one's thighs. The right one more than the left. I can't say why that is. Just feels heavier, and harder.

That slow, sinking feeling, just beneath my collarbone—burdens of the heart accumulate right there.

Intrusive thoughts reside in the nape of your neck. Cold and cunning, they tend to creep up whenever happiness is on the move, approaching slowly, shyly.

Toes are bent with anxiety. You don't even notice until you unclench, and then you are like, ah, so that's what it feels like to relax.

Jaws tend to live in great fear. Fear of falling, failure, finance, and forgetting. They tense under the weight, making teeth grind all night long.

Anger toils and troubles, boils and bubbles in your throat, inflamed, bright red, infected.

Sins are stored in your hair—the split ones, the exhausted ends, breaking from guilt unspoken. Under the hose, I rub my head with soap until white foam puffs up and slips down my neck. I watch black hairs swirl and dance and go down the drain. My sins lead a fun life after they leave me.

GREENER PASTURES

According to Harbir, the guy who occupied my mattress before me
has moved on to greener pastures. Literally. Hari Singh now works as
a shepherd on the island of Sardinia, guardian of the local black
sheep, pecore nere. He's working independently—a free agent, no
coordinators controlling him whatsoever. I wish I was a freelancer,
too. I think coordination is not really working in my favor.

PECORE NERE

As a Black Sardinian sheep, from the moment you are born—hooves
first, slick with warm blood, amniotic fluid, skins and goo—certain
things are expected from you. What follows is the pecore nere code
of conduct, as documented in their rich and varied oral history.

1. Stand out. Strength of head and heart are expected. Stand
   your ground. Don't budge. Believe in the essence of black
   sheepness. Your thick wool, rich jet black or chocolate
   brown, may be soft, but your souls are solid.

2. Always remember: the family is the family is the family. The
   herd is everything. Where do you come from? The herd.
   Where will you return to? The eternal herd in the sky.
   Fragrant herbs aplenty. Omnia ab uno—everything from the
   herd. Individuality in community; this is it.

3. Our ears may be small, but we share uncanny hearing abilities with our faraway friends, the lynxes. You may confess your sins in our presence. We will keep a secret. In fact, we will carry it to our graves. The incessant chatter and gossip of the white sheep is of no interest to a true pecora nera.

4. We believe in equality: all black sheep are horned. No gender division. Equal rights. That is what we stand for.

5. Be your own sheep. Don't be someone else's sheep. We don't believe in the concept of ownership. Sheep were among the first animals to be domesticated by humans, around 10,000 BC in Mesopotamia. Having witnessed the wild mouflon incarcerated and skinned alive, we resisted. And we will keep on resisting. We were living on these grounds centuries before humans could even walk the earth in an upright position. We only pretend to be shepherded, just to gain valuable protection and food. We scam the shepherds. You should, too. That is our advice.

EVERYBODY'S LOOKING
FOR SOMETHING

The blood-red walls contain me like a sardine, preserved in my own juices. Had ONE traveled the world and the seven seas before settling here, as a home for brown men with tiny shovels? Everybody's looking for something. Of that I am sure. Everybody's looking for something.

EUROPE: THE
TOWELETTES INITIATIVE

"Europe, I have been wondering: can you change the law?"

"Change the law? Whatever do you mean, Happy?"

"Change, as in make different rules. New rules. Make the old ones disappear."

"Well, up to a certain extent . . . Let me put it this way: I can give input on a suggestion for a change."

"Sounds rather . . . vague."

"Believe me, it is."

"Hm."

"Which law did you have in mind?"

"If you wanted to give input on a suggestion for a change, say, regarding who is invited into Europe and who will have to stay out— how would you do that?"

"First, I'd have to draw up a report on a proposal for an amendment to a 'legislative text' presented by the Commission, the only institution empowered to initiate legislation."

"How does that work exactly?"

"I have to get the opinions of my family, which is always a pain. I will take into consideration my family's opinion and those of countless experts in all the different fields of European law and policy, you see. Then come the questionnaires—I have to tick certain boxes. The boxes I tick are the suggestions for change."

"What happens next?"

"Well, whatever those in power want, really. My suggestions for change are only that: suggestions."

"Really? But doesn't your voice, like, count double?"

"No."

"But you're Europe?"

"It doesn't work that way, I'm afraid. Not anymore. Everything has become so bureaucratic. Some don't even know my face anymore."

"I'm sorry to hear that."

"Thank you. I try to repress it as much as I can, but . . ."

"Well, can you at least give input on a suggestion to possibly maybe change your role?"

"You are sweet. I could. But it would never work. I'll give you an example: I once lead an initiative to provide welcome packages for the new arrivals. The packages would have included stuff like towels, nice toiletries, various high-caloric Central European snacks, socks, fresh shirts or dresses or maybe even baby blankets. We had it all worked out, lots of donors on board already. I was quite excited.

"My proposal didn't get through, though. The only thing that got approved were those disposable towelettes monogrammed with my initials. At least they're scented. Sicilian lemon, not the generic off-brand lemon you get on airplanes."

"I didn't get any towelettes."

"You didn't? Are you sure?"

"No. Never. Would have loved to get some. Sounds like a nice idea. To wipe the dust of the journey . . ."

"Off your hands, yes. I'm sorry. Sometimes they forget . . . and there are delivery squeezes all the time. The towelettes are made in Albania in this little manufactory. Oh well."

"So, no changing of the rules at all?"

"As I said, from my experience, it just isn't going to work out. Bureaucracy is a bitch. I'm sorry . . . that was inappropriate of me. And I believe also sexist."

IMAGINE

"Harbir, did you imagine it this way?"

"What?"

"This. Europe. Italy."

"Mhh. I try not to imagine things. Only leads to disappointment. You'll be happier if you don't hope for too much in the first place."

"Imagining is all I do."

"Ha. Yes. I know. You imagine too much, Happy Singh. Think too much. Attach too much meaning to things."

We are both quiet for a moment, watching Zhivago soak his socks in a pink plastic bowl with utmost care. The water turns gray as he keeps swirling the socks around in the water.

"Happy, you wanted to know whether I imagined it this way. I didn't."

"So, you did imagine *something*."

"I didn't. But I did have an image in my mind . . ."

"That is literally what imagining is, Harbir."

"Anyway, this is what I saw: a white house on a hill, a Fiat Panda, my wife and me, and two little boys. They were playing soccer. Fast runners."

"Wow. That sounds nice. Was your beard glistening in the sun? Was Guru Nanak Dev presiding in the sky above your white house?"

"I will never tell you anything again, idiot."

"No, come back! Harbir! I think your dream is perfect. Maybe one day it will come true!"

TEST

I lie awake at night and do personality tests on my mobile.

What is your love language?

Myers-Briggs Type Indicator

What boss type are you?

Are you experienced?

TypeFinder

What your favorite food says about you.

Suicidal disposition according to rising sign.

Career Finder

What your favorite food says about your sexuality

When will you find love?

What's your perfect date?

Are you a high heels, boots, or sneakers girl?

When will you die—and do you want to know?

Big Five Assessment

Can you be my lucky star?

I can be so lucky

Lucky lucky lucky

In Love

(I haven't written anything in a long time.)

UNFORESEEN INCIDENT

There is a whisper through the grapevine, along the growing tunnels and porta potties: an accident with one of the harvesters and a state-of-the-art machine. A Romanian machinist has not been seen since. The Polish suppliers told the Moldavian storage managers about it and they had in turn passed on the information to us General Farm Workers. We don't know exactly what happened; it's all very hush-hush.

ATTENTION:

Next Tuesday the farm will be closed for a federal safety inspection.

Half day for all. 6–12 a.m.

Exceptional one time only. Stay in your residences.

New safety protocols to be implemented upon reopening.

THE CARAVAN KITCHEN

The Caravan Kitchen is a brand-new institution: Zhivago has just invented it. Open every Sunday, he intends to feed all the General Workers a homemade meal to boost morale and facilitate team building.

He got the idea when an old caravan showed up in Paradise Square, featuring a fully operational kitchen with two gas stoves and a tiny little oven. The caravan is home to three new arrivals, additional hands for picking season: Amir, Nas, and Harkan. Zhiv convinced them to let him use the kitchen for a communal project. Luckily, the new guys are up for sharing their space; the idea of real food seems to greatly outweigh the invasion of privacy.

Zhiv prefers to cook alone. We organize the ingredients together, though. Organize, as in we don't exactly buy them. Produce comes to us gladly and of their own free will. They know their destiny will be delicious. Even the chicken putters toward us happily, plump breasts swaying, beak greedily following our small trail of grains. Zhivago has to do the killing part, though. I never could stomach the task of wringing a delicate chicken neck and hearing the bones crack like fragile twigs underneath violent feet.

The scent of ketjap manis, cumin, and roasting chicken flesh wafts through the caravan's open doors. It is the hottest day of the summer, probably around 113 degrees, but Zhivago intends to stick to the plan. He is stubborn like that. On the menu for opening day is a Surinamese chicken sandwich; *very Indian, actually*, he explains, with its flavorful curry sauce.

MEAL OF THE DAY

Surinamese chicken curry sandwich

with a side of black locust blossom fritters, cabbage relish and fig chutney.

Special offer: Happy-made nimbu pani

THE RULES OF HOSPITALITY

Before the Caravan Kitchen, there was the Night of Board Games & Discussions and the Music & Movie Exchange—no one had turned up except for Harbir and myself, and that was only because these events took place in our container. The Caravan Kitchen is Zhivago's first real and very tangible success. Might have something to do with the fact that it involves free food.

"Here you go!" I am done cutting the cabbage.

Zhivago looks at my cutting board under moist, lowered brows.

"Once more, with feeling."

It's hard to breathe in here, with all the cooking steams and juices evaporating in the heat.

"Are you kidding me? This is as fine as they come. I am definitely not cutting it again."

"It needs to be super fine, Happy. Like this: tiny and delicate. It's for relish. Who can swallow these thick brick-like pieces? Respect your customer, always."

Outside, the other workers are joining Harbir, waiting for the Caravan Kitchen to open, wet towels slung over their heads to help them cool down. Most are dozing in the shadows, letting the ants crawl over their legs; too tired to be bothered, they choose peaceful coexistence.

"What customers? They are just a bunch of freeloaders."

Zhiv looks up at me, smiling.

"They are my guests, and I am their host. There are very simple rules to hospitality. A true gift is given without question, in the most perfect way deemed appropriate and possible, and without asking for anything in return."

I feel a little strange whenever he looks at me so intently with those brown-green eyes (dirty pond at noon).

HAPPY TV: BE THE CHANGE YOU WANT TO SEE IN THE WORLD

ARJUN

Of course I want change. Change every things. Is my motto. What did he say? *Be the change you want to see* or somethin'? Yeah. Guess it's true. Nothing gets happening for you unless you make it happening yourself. Used to make me angry—exhausting, man!! Seriously. Now, I just accept. Maybe better: no one to mess up for you either. I don't like destiny destiny pray pray. So, yeah, do the change. Seed the change. Eat the change. Shit the change. Make new change grow again from the smelly shit, layer by layer, composting, fermenting, percolating, till it's all changed all over; paradise and all that. Talking about shitting, when's this lunch thing ready you think?

TARSEM

I do like order, though. I like rules to follow. I used to be a keen wedding dancer back at home—check out this video . . . got it right here . . . wait, sorry, slow network . . . here we go . . . dude, I know right? Lifetime ago.

I enjoy working along those tidy rows of radishes, seeing every man in front of me completing the same task I do, at a slightly different rhythm and pace. Even if it's the same old ugly behinds I'm looking at. I like counting *exactly* eight radishes to a bunch. I revel in reaching my daily target, and I'm deeply satisfied if what's dirty gets cleaned, what's creased is smoothed, and if what seems uncontrollable, unsurmountable, chaotic, becomes structured and manageable—*pretty*. I used to braid my daughter's hair, too. Excelled at it. Her name's Gulwinder. Need to use Amla oil to smooth the strands first, that's the secret. Your mother, too? Oh, nice, man. Good name. She'll start school this year. This is a picture of her, see . . . next to me seated on the tractor—I'm teaching her to drive, ha. She has grown so much since that pic though—yeah, had to sell that tractor, too . . . I haven't seen her in almost two years.

AMIR

You don't know about it? Hardeep's Underground Paneer Production? Been living under a rock? I mean. It's probably just tall tales . . . but if it *were* true, this is how it would have come about: Hardeep came to Italy about five years ago. The agents took him via Algeria. Scammers. Abandoned him. He had to hide out for months. Actually, like, *starving*. Got jaundice and all—miserable, man. Stuck. Then, he meets this guy Aahan; good fella that one. Has connections to Italy.

Fake ID, voila—boards a flight to Roma. Starts working as a bergamini straight away. Cows, water buffaloes, goats—lots of experience back home in Punjab. Hard work though. And paid badly, very badly—you know how it is.

Hardeep misses palak paneer—we all do, right—and he never wants to starve again. His fellow workers, all Punjabis: same same.

And so, all of the sudden, there's a leak in one of the milk tanks. A few liters mysteriously disappear. Few more. Trickling, seeping, bit by bit. Lemons keep vanishing from a plantation . . . wild boars developed an appetite for lemons, see. And here we go: Hardeep's Underground Paneer Production is born. Flourishing business. You can order via Whatsapp. 2-3 business days to process order. Anyways, if it *were* true . . .

NAS

On that orange plantation down South, Amir and I—it's grim down South that's what I've always been saying but Amir was like: *nah they pay well, almost* double, *dude, have you done the math*, and I was like, *nah, man, been hearing bad things*, but he was like, *what are you, are you like, scared, man*, and I was like, *never been scared in my life, don't have a scared bone in my body, I am a noble descendant from a long line of ancient warriors, are you, tiny insignificant motherfucking motherfucker without balls and brains, are you trying to argue with me?*—so, but, yeah, tike, we went in the end.

Blood oranges. And it turned out just as bad as I'd predicted, of course—'cause that's who I am, right, I'm a truthteller, a fighter, without a scared bone in my body, mind you . . . anyway, what was I saying. Yeah. Revolt. That's what's been happening down there. When we arrived—everyone but Amir and myself was from Mali, right. Don't know how the coordinators decide these things, like, have you ever wondered—how they place Romanians, Moldavians, Moroccans, North-Indians, Pakistanis, Malinese, Sudanese . . . seems to follow an intricate plan, doesn't it? Do you feel it seems to follow an intricate plan, this *coordination*? Or is it just a big bunch of bullshit? Might be the case that it's just *bullshit*, man.

One fine day—Friday, April 21st, I remember exactly—some friends from Mali were promenading through town, peacefully, minding their own business—food run, bags of rice, rather handsome eggplants, red onions . . . became quite a fan of tiguadege na by the way, *very* peanutty, *extremely* delicious—and then, out of nowhere, conjuring a reason out of thin air (*are you looking at me funny?* that kinda thing), some locals started a fight. Seems it got out of hand. Kicking those already lying on the ground, unmoving—kicking people's heads, no less—*no*. Gotta draw a line somewhere. There's an *ethos* to a fight, you see. Otherwise the world is just . . . mayhem. Might call it assault rather than a fight then. One newspaper did. *Racist Attack* and all that. Two of our friends got injured badly. Didn't call an ambulance at first though because—*papers*, right—'twas a close call. *Very* close call. We had to get a doctor in the end. Only deaf in one ear. Lucky, really. They'd been working down there for more than three years at that point, and they had to take a lot of slurs, some insults, some pushing, shoving, vaffanculos, same old . . . finally, after this, guys from Mali decided they'd had enough. *Basta*. Hence, the protests. Mobilized *many* friends. Rest is history. You've probably read it in the papers, right? Now, they've formed their own cooperative, acquired some land—yeah, they actually did!

Legally—selling lovely *organic* produce to well-off gente in Rome. Yoghurt is excellent, man. Nice and fatty. Creamy and dreamy. Reminds me of home. Almost water buffalo quality.

I will text them. Ask whether they can send some over! Zhiv would like that, too.

Yeah, Amir and I, we did lay low during the protests. Didn't read about us in the papers, did you? We weren't scared, no. Told you. Not a scared bone in my . . . just assumed it was . . . more fore-sighted and like, diligent . . . to remain at the back of the action. Didn't mean we don't support it. Fully support it. Honest. All for the revolution, man. Fully in favor of it.

SUKHA

I don't know what you want me to say. I'm too hungry. Let me sweat in peace. Come back once I've eaten. What's Surinamese when it's at home, anyways? When will this sandwich thingy be done? Did he say?

DEEP NAVEL PEOPLE

I am floating in the lake like a starfish, naked and blooming. The universe is pouring its condensed light into my navel. The light and the lake are cleaning my navel. My navel is usually quite smelly and I must confess I like the scent, and I wonder if other deep navel people feel the same way. Deep navel people, of course, are deeper than shallow navel people, who are shallow. I laugh out loud, swallowing moldy lake water, coughing and spitting. The spit-lake droplets multiply and turn into cabbage-white butterflies with grenades attached to their backs, exploding into a myriad of pieces when they touch the surface of the water. I find suddenly that I can swim, though I never did learn. I feel like I could cross an entire ocean, taking on the form of a dolphin, an ancient whale, or a hermit crab.

A hermit crab can walk for miles and miles—its whole life is about walking, really . . . and it's got . . . it's got its, what's it called . . . its shell, right? A mobile home.

I never told you, did I?

Or did I?

I might have, right?

I've been having these dreams. About a giant frostbitten foot, a foot that turns into a mountainscape, and then the whole world is infected and dies . . .

Nadeesh. Stuck between Europe and Asia, forever and ever, ever.

Why would he put on those shit sneakers, anyway . . .

Have you met an Amrit, here in Italy? Have you seen an Amrit, anywhere? No? OK. Was only wondering. Was only wandering.

Hey, Zhiv?

Where is Zhivago? One moment, we were sitting by the container, smoking, the next, he was gone.

A big vibration. Can you feel it, too? The poplar trees are shaking their heads in unison. Bowing down deep and coming up for air. A storm is rising. Inside or outside of me? Boundaries are a little blurry right now.

A swooshing of sorts is underway. Vertigo will prevail, that's for sure. My mouth feels numb.

In the porta potty, I lean my head against the wall. My belly emits a low rumbling. I massage it in circular motions, like the old ladies in the village did with newborns suffering from colic. They used simple cooking oil, and it worked like magic.

WHAT ZHIVAGO TOLD ME

Zhivago wasn't born in a small village, like me, but underneath the amber lights of a big city. He wasn't born in a hospital, but on the streets, not at the hands of an experienced aunty, just his mother all on her own.

At first, he didn't cry, but waited, waited, and waited, eyes closed, face crumpled up like an angry little raisin, until his mother got scared and shook him—and then, finally, he breathed, screaming a blue murder that made people turn in their sleep all the way on the other side of the city.

What he saw, when he opened his eyes for the first time: a disc, yellow and bright, and his mother's face, dark, exhausted, teary, full luscious lips that he would inherit later on, but in the beginning his mouth had been tiny, clenched, disappointed. He would have thought there'd be more beauty on the other side, more people awaiting him, and maybe a house, too. But for his first years, this street corner had to do.

AMBIKA: ON CARRYING THINGS

I, too, am a bag, a skin, a room, a container.

I contain torso, arm, leg, lip, teeth, skin, toes, see-through fingernails and glassy lashes, flesh, and fresh enthusiastic blood, wrapped around a tiny zealous heart. A sea of amniotic fluids, unbeknownst to men, a Mariana Trench of secrets and possible complications and unforeseen growth potential.

My skin forms a carrier bag and thus

I carry.

Hard to think and do otherwise.

And then:

Little legs wrapped around my middle, little hands slapping my chest because it makes a noise that delights you, my hip pushed out and up, as if for a dance in suspended animation—

Now, I am not just a carrier bag, but a sofa, a plush seating opportunity, a kinetic sculpture, an unstinting fridge, a horse, a scooter, and a helicopter, a spirited singer, akin to Sade or Lata Mangeshkar, an untiring reciter of stories, an ignorer of intolerable conditions in general and about six ounces of pee on my pants in particular; a soft machine, made just for you, if you want me to be.

I read the same lines over and over again:

A merry jelly jellyfish

I shimmy in the sea

No other fish can shimmy just as perfectly as me.

I read these lines aloud so often, with grace and conviction and humor, while having you press down on my lap, warm and moist and tender, breathing into your hair, that I begin reciting them aloud when I am alone, too, walking through the market looking for flour and alma extract (my hair, it keeps falling out), while writing emails, while listening to my mother-in-law and Gul dislike each other word-lessly, while listening to Jiten's tales of incompetent colleagues, while sitting in the gurdwara, wearing a bright blue chunni, letting the Kiran wash through my closed eyes, and in the car, music turned up so loud I am allowed to scream *jellyfish* like an incandes-cent threat—their tentacles can inject poison from thousands of microscopic barbed stingers, turning skin angry and red, and, if they're feeling especially powerful that day, causing temporary paral-ysis, and wouldn't that be something, I think, as I drive, and the monsoon rains turn furious, and I can't see a thing through the wind-screen, one wiper is limp, much like my arm after a long day, and I keep hitting the mud with my wheels made of fire.

FATEHPAL: ON LOVE

"You know what Fatehpal means, right?"

"Here we go. *The one who protects and is victorious.*"

"*Mighty victorious protector.* Yes. I protect my family. I care for them."

"How do you know how to care for them?"

"What do you mean?"

"Well . . . I can feel what other people feel. I put myself in their position and—it, like, physically hurts. If someone gets hurt in a movie, I have to avert my eyes. I have to switch it off. It's too much. But if I try to do something about it in real life, comfort someone . . . I rarely know what to do, or what to say."

"OK. Well—there are some things. Basic things. Food, water, a place to sleep. I give them that, for starters. A house. A house is important. For the future. A garden. Vacations are important, too. The sea. Wander along a beach. I never knew they'd need this, but they do, they definitely do. Collect shells and buckets full of crabs. Carry your children through a rain shower, take off their sandals, wash their feet.

"I also gave the girls the Barbie cruise ship. It came with a mixer on deck. For milkshakes, you know? To be honest, what they truly love is those cardboard boxes I bring home from the factory . . . We should have just given them the empty box of the cruise ship."

"OK. I mean—but what about love?"

"Love? Yes, of course, love. I love them."

"But how do you know that's what love is?"

"I care for them, don't I? I brought them home from the hospital and purchased all the things they need. I got up at night when they were scared, brought them to school, and helped them with their homework for as long as I could still help them . . ."

"Your children, yes. Unconditional love. But what about Frida?"

"Frida, she is my wife. Of course I love her. Although, she's making it difficult for me to love her and for the love to stay the same. Sometimes there's just this gaping angry hole where my love used to be . . . She gets me so mad, you wouldn't believe it."

"I understand. You do get angry sometimes. That's—"

"Yes. And she gets angry, too. Mostly, my anger starts with her anger. And then it multiplies. You should see her fury—her face . . . it gets all . . . scrunched up. Piercing blue eyes. But when she's happy, her eyes are so beautiful, like Princess Di's, no kidding. I still can't believe she picked me."

"You picked each other."

"Yes, we did. But we were young. Way too young. And there's always a price for going against your family. Anyways—why are you asking me all these love, love questions? Why are you thinking so much? Is there someone . . . ?"

"No, no. Not at all."

"They are treating you OK, right? Happy? You would say if—You just need to say the word."

"All good, Fatehpal. All good."

FRANZ AND ODILE:
SO, WE'RE IN LOVE?

So, we're in love? asks Franz.

We'll see soon enough, replies Odile.

FROM WHERE I'M STANDING

Seven months of working at the radish farm, and I still haven't worked my way up to the top. I am not even sure there is a top to work up to. If there is one, I can't see it from where I'm standing. The top seems distant and dangerous, eerie mountaintops marking the Iranian border. Hidden behind the fog and smoke and mirrors. Up so far you cannot see. You are in danger of losing your mind, staring at the top for too long.

Behind me, I can barely make out the silhouettes of my old plans. An ancient city lost in a sandstorm. Buried alive.

NOKIA 9310

Recently, Zhivago has been spending a lot of time on his phone. It's an old Nokia, so all he can do is call and text. He is squatting outside the growing tent, still in his work wear, hands dirty from soil, and talks fast, gesticulating, serious, intent. I don't understand anything he says.

HARBIR IS ALWAYS TEXTING

little one, how r things at ur end?

little one, i miss your voice.

little one, harvest is done. days getting shorter. my back is killing me. how are things at ur end?

little one, a song u might like.

the weather is colder now. miss you, little one.

little one, just got the news. how's your father? why did he walk out there on his own? u need to tell me these things. i can help. ok? don't keep quiet. u r always quiet. keep things to urself . . .

little one, ur worries are my worries now.

little one, i will bring him to italy for hip surgery once things improve. be hopeful. all will be well.

little one, the 2 idiots like to talk about their feelings. dreamz and feelingz all day all nite.

littel one, how r u? hope all iz well. v tired tday. can't keep eyes open. box giant freezer not made for living. counting days til i get to c u. which i hope is soon.

little one, i cannot believe it hasn't arrived yet. don't they know u need it to work? take sukhpal with u. and make sure u tell them i am ur fiance.

little one, will get u over here once things improve. v soon.
praying for ur health and happiness, always.

little one, winter sadness in the box. everyone non-stop coughing.
happy talking in his sleep.

little one, r u ok? have not heard in a while . . .

little one, ok, will call you choti from now on. choti, the great, is
that better? :)

hey choti, shall i call u?

i will call u.

RISO AMARO

Zhiv and I are squatting in front of our container, eating stolen peaches
and watching a clip of *Riso Amaro* on my phone. It's a super old
movie, part of the research *for our cause*, as Zhivago had said, amber-
colored peach juice trickling down his chin.

The premise of *Riso Amaro*, in many ways, is an interesting rever-
sal of our situation. Centuries ago, in the fifties, Italians themselves
had been irregolari. North and South, on and off the books, union
and non-union; age-old categories, universal indeed.

The film is *neorealismo*, Zhivago had said, a gangster movie, and
a love story, too. A love triangle, just like in *Bande à part*. And yet
again involving a heist, or its aftermath.

The female rice pickers—regolari and irregolari—are wrestling in the muddy waters of the fields; grabbing, pulling each other's hair, falling, pushing, and slapping with real rage and vigor. I love the stylized fights of Bruce Lee, and adore the make-believe shoot-outs in *Bande à part*, but this here is very much like a fight in real life would be. Real rage is messy.

CONTAINERING

There're two perfectly good yellow peppers; a Styrofoam package containing twelve eggs, six of which are broken, yolks and egg whites oozing out onto a box of expired frozen pizzas ("Greek Style"); a limp leek with yellow outer leaves; a bunch of iceberg lettuces sweating in their plastic packaging; a tin of peanuts ("Oriental Seasoning"), probably expired; a whole lot of prepackaged salads with corn and kidney beans ("Mexicana"); expired pots of cheesecake ("New York!"); a watermelon so ripe it exploded when they threw it in the trash, juice leaking down onto a bunch of mushy corncobs and glasses of glossy dark amarenata cherries; a quarter of an expired pecorino, crumbly and snow-white; as well as mini Gouda cheese rolls with images of a blond Dutch girl on them; a net of moldy lemons; a stale loaf of ciabatta, soaked with melon juice; some scruffy beans; and a plastic package with the cartoony image of a man in a turban saying, in swirly mock-handwritten letters, "Ready-made naan bread, garlic flavor."

RAT DROPPINGS

I google *rat droppings size difference mouse shit*

Mouse poop is considerably smaller than rat poop, often not measuring longer than one-quarter of an inch, while rat poop is often a one-half inch or larger. Rat poop is also shinier than mouse poop, which could be an easy way for you to tell the difference between these two infestations.

SMALLPOX VACCINATION SCAR

Zhiv has been collecting official-looking documents in a green planting box underneath his bed. He keeps reading, annotating, shuffling, and sorting through them, usually very early in the mornings, when he thinks no one is watching.

I'm awake and trying to get a glimpse. Lots and lots of minuscule numbers. Big stamps. Some of the papers are yellowed, some are folded, having slid out of envelopes.

He stuffs them back inside and gets dressed. His brown skin looks soft. The cold morning light bounces off his shoulders. There is a circular scar from the smallpox vaccination on his upper left arm. My brothers bore the same mark: the skin is lighter around the violent puncture; it looks like the rays of the sun.

COHABITATION

Winter has reached Latina.

We have one portable radiator to share between us: exquisite, hypnotic iridescent hot-glint half-god of heat. Highly coveted. Can only warm one person at a time.

No hot water, though. The pipes are frozen.

Harbir, Zhiv, and I, we've been living in the container for seven months. *Cohabitation,* Zhivago says, *asks for mutual respect, seeking peaceful solutions to conflicts at all times.*

Signs of said cohabitation: like beavers who can't shake that primeval urge to build a dam, we carried all kinds of stuff into the caravan—thick blankets, old pots and boxes, empty tins (predominantly Serbian bean stew from a local discounter, filling and warm, at least—we saved them as containers for things—what exactly? Flowers? Cash? What do you ever save things for?), tools for Harbir to repair things, and an old boom box splattered with paint in all kinds of colors. I imagine it belonged to a painter, who used it to play songs that fed his imagination; we found it on the street, still working perfectly well.

A NIGHT IN THE
GROWING TUNNELS

The early radishes are sown in mid-February: the Malaga Violet, a Polish variety, earthier and milder than the cherry radish. A far more interesting leading lady, I'd say. When the first seedlings start to show their light green tips, tentatively, at the end of March, the nights can still get frosty. I feel responsible, for my rows in particular, since I was the one who brought them into this world. Thus, remembering my nights spent out on the cabbage fields as a child—the comfort, the coziness, warm limbs, the cold nose, the morning chai brought out by Gul—I take out my sleeping bag and bring along all of Gul's scarves, too.

The embroidered dupattas look nice spread out upon the earth. They are light enough not to hurt the seedlings, nor do they apply too much pressure to the plant, weighing them down—not just any fabric could achieve this balance. Gul's scarves are perfect for the job: empathic, flexible, and resilient.

I lay down in the small patch in between the rows and watch the sky darken through the silver ceiling of the tunnel. I hear a plunge, a peck, see crow's feet hop along the foil, and sing a rough evening song for me and my seedlings. It gets chilly fast, but I am snug in my sleeping bag. We all fall asleep in no time.

DIGNITY AND DECORUM

Dignity and decorum of living spaces: yes / no / maybe.

Please tick the appropriate box.

THE CONTAINER CLUB

Zhivago suggested we come together for weekly meetings to "better our situation." Keen on projecting scope and eminence, he's christened the meeting The Container Club. The General Workers start trickling in, unilaterally complaining about the smell. It might have been the air perfume in the scent Spring Peach I bought off the Chinese lady down by the road. The scent does have a sickly-sweet note lurking at the bottom—but it's better than the usual container must. Without Zhivago's promise of free snacks and booze, they likely wouldn't have shown up at all.

ZHIVAGO'S SPEECH

"The production of Italian pecorino cheese is almost entirely in Sikh hands—see? This is the cheese . . . can you just help me out here, hold this for a moment . . . yes.

"Now, what would the cheese be without the hand to hold it? Exactly. It would fall!

"And that's just an example. Local agriculture all over Europe, and, indeed, Italian food culture, is highly dependent on immigrant labor. Thing is, this immigrant labor is often performed by undocumented immigrants—so called irregolari—such as the people present in this room. Wildly underpaid, working for as little as one euro per hour. The structures of agricultural employment are criminal. This much we know to be true.

"Imagine Europe without migrant labor. Especially in the agricultural sector: no radishes, no oranges, no pecorino, no Grana Padano, no strawberries, no unseasonal raspberries, no cheap asparagus, no big fat lemons, in fact, no Gucci leather handbags either—Europe would be deprived of its everyday luxury, stripped of food privilege and its favorite delectable consumer goods. Products would be so expensive, the system as we know it would simply collapse. Supermarket shelves would be bare and empty! Deserted. Just tinned stew imported from Serbia. Imagine! Just picture it.

"Europe would be nothing without us. Nothing. Desires: unmet. Cravings: ignored. Calls: declined. There'd be riots. I'm telling you.

"*Riot* is the key word here. We need an uprising. And the first step, always, is a protest. Bringing attention to the very thing that has been silenced.

"So, the situation is clear. Things need to change. The old radish needs to die so that the new radish may be born. So that *we* may be reborn, in free and independent labor.

"The question is, What do we want? Where do we want to go from here? What are the means we have—"

At that point of the speech, just as we'd practiced it (many times in fact), I press play on the boom box: "Gonna Fly Now" from the *Rocky* soundtrack blares from the speakers, filling our home with a sense of momentousness and magnitude. I see a hard and blazing look in the eyes of the General Farm Workers. Some clapping and cheer.

Zhiv gives me a thumbs-up. I smile.

EUROPE

Europe pulls her blue pashmina over her shoulders and retreats into a fat blue-tinged cloud that had been stubbornly floating above the farm all day. She scrolls through her phone and looks at old childhood pictures. They are sad and blurry and make her feel even worse. Her nervous stomach flares up again. A sour taste swells up in her mouth. This always happens when she is criticized.

THE TINY SHOVEL MANIFESTO

The tiny shovel plays an elemental role both in the birth and the harvest of the radish; it is the basic tool for every radish worker.

I take the tiny shovel out of a box by the entrance of the growing tents. A black plastic bin not unlike a garbage bin but filled with other tiny shovels. Mine has a handle made of lacquered green wood, but where the paint splinters, it's light brown. The shovel itself is made of steel, boasting a sharply pointed end, to dig and cut and toil and pull.

It can be a weapon, if you will, with the right amount of vigor and determination.

Each of the eleven men working this morning holds a tiny shovel of their own, pressed firmly into their fists, shoveling tiny holes for the tiny seedlings and digging birthing tunnels for the radishes.

This is what we see of the shovel. But what does the shovel actually think? What does it feel?

The shovels are screaming in unison, I swear. They are forming an underground choir, a meandering shovel manifesto. Just press your ears to the earth and listen:

> *SHARP SHARP SHARP DIG DIG DIG DOWN INTO*
> *EARTHLAND,*
> *MY FRIEND*
>
> *You saw me glistening once*
> *(in silence)*
> *Retreading morosely into*
> *voluptuous dirt*
>
> *Push me deeper into*
> *Worm Shit*
> *(into silence)*
> *Don't mind me pulling out some clots*
> *along the way*
>
> *Evanescent incandescent green*
> *Believe me*

We can do this
I swear

The men of the shovel
The men of the sweat
We do need your bodies
Your energy imprint
And rise without fail

The workers united
In power they stand
They carry us proudly
And shout one by one

SHARP SHARP SHARP DIG DIG DIG DEEP DEEP DEEP
HOLD ON, MY FRIEND

All shovels are Communists. Their dreamland is Kerala, where the Communist Party has been reigning for centuries and both food and climate are mild and accommodating. The shovels dream a collective dream: of an Edison light bulb and a Paleozoic rock in close embrace, swaying to the faint tune of "Tiny Dancer."

Whatever the meaning, I cannot say.

MEETING MINUTES: HERE'S THE PLAN

ITEM 1: The Situation

Zhivago elaborates on the importance of Sikh workers for the Italian agricultural industry and suggests revolution.

ITEM 2: Uprising

A worker uprising is in order to better our situation!

ITEM 3: Means to achieve said uprising

First step: Protest!

Questions: Who will do what? We need to organize with general workers from neighboring farms, gain critical numbers, form committees for different tasks, etc.

Second step: Death to the Radish!

Third step: Radish may be reborn in free and independent labor— founding something like a cooperative to sell our own produce, also, small food place, stall on Roman markets (?), or work with pecore nere and henceforward become a movie star (Happy).

USKI ROTI

"How long do you think she will wait?"

"She'll wait until he comes," I say.

Zhivago and I are sitting at our usual spot on the container threshold, watching *Uski Roti* on my phone.

Every day, Balo, a Punjabi housewife, is preparing lunch for her husband, a bus driver, who spends most of his time with his mistress in a nearby town. Balo is waiting for him at the bus stop with warm rotis—except for that one time, when she is late. And from there, the plot unravels. A quiet, hypnotic kind of unraveling.

My battery is almost dead. Phone dies in no time ever since I dropped it into the porta potty last week.

We keep watching Balo waiting at the deserted bus stop as darkness descends onto the dusty soil. She rests her head on her knees; her eyes are wide open. A gust of wind. Billows of sand rise, obscuring our view. My phone battery is at 2 percent.

Zhivago turns toward me. There is a smear of aubergine in his hair—he had roasted one over the gas cooker for dinner.

"He won't come, will he?"

"He might not, no."

DEATH TO THE RADISH

He is drawing each letter in bright green lacquer with great care, biting his lips as he does whenever he is concentrating really hard:

DEATH TO THE RADISH

The word *radish* is accentuated in tomato red with glossy drops of "blood," dripping down the *R* and the *H*—a powerful embellishment he adds as an afterthought.

Zhivago steps back and surveys his work, contentedly.

RADIO LATINA: PROTEST OF THE RADISH PICKERS

On the day of the protest, for the first time ever, I am interviewed by an actual reporter. The journalist is young, around my age. Her hair is short and she is wearing black motorcycle boots and black leggings with an intricate pattern of white skulls. She presses the microphone into the small space beneath my nose, looking intent. Her delicate face carries a grave expression that I try to mirror and meet with adequate respect.

> **RADIO LATINA:** Buongiorno. Is English OK? Who are you and why are you here today?

HAPPY SINGH SONI: Sure, it is. Well, as you can see, I am part of the protest.

RADIO LATINA: Where are you currently working?

HAPPY SINGH SONI: Radish farm. The big one. You must have passed it on the way.

RADIO LATINA: I know where it is, yes. I am from around here. How long have you been staying in Italy? And where are you originally from?

HAPPY SINGH SONI: One and a half years now, almost to the day. I am from Punjab, India. A small village—you wouldn't know it if I told you its name. It is close to the city of Jalandhar.

RADIO LATINA: May I ask, are you here with an official working permit? It is OK if you do not wish to answer.

HAPPY SINGH SONI: I do not wish to answer.

RADIO LATINA: OK, OK. That's fine. I can imagine. Your living conditions, what are they like? Where and how do you live? At the farm?

HAPPY SINGH SONI: I am sharing a room—or rather a container. My roommates are Harbir, the tall one over there, the one with the turban, and Zhivago, who organized this whole thing. He is over there with Tarsem. They . . .

RADIO LATINA: You live in a container? Did I get that right? For how long now?

HAPPY SINGH SONI: Nine months . . . I think. Yes, roundabout.

RADIO LATINA: You spent the winter at the farm, too.

HAPPY SINGH SONI: Yes.

RADIO LATINA: Do you have access to heating, running hot water? Regular meals?

HAPPY SINGH SONI: There is a portable heater that we share. We take turns who can use it. It warms up one corner of the container at a time. There is no hot water, no, but it sometimes runs, yes. The hose is temperamental, though. You have to give it a proper shake if it's blocked.

As for the meals, well—not as regular as they could be. Not as regular as at home. Rather irregular, to be honest. But Zhivago is an excellent cook. I think he could open a restaurant. Maybe he will one day. He started the Caravan Kitchen a while back—a new special every Sunday. Mostly variations of the same chicken sandwich, which is my all-time favorite.

RADIO LATINA: He seems resourceful. You probably have to be, right? But no proper heating, no hot water—you know you do have a right to have access to all these things, right? Do you pay rent for the accommodation?

HAPPY SINGH SONI: Yes. They take it off our daily pay directly. We get twenty euros per day. Well, minus the fee for the coordinators. And minus rent.

RADIO LATINA: Who are the coordinators?

HAPPY SINGH SONI: I . . . I do not wish to answer. And, truthfully, I don't really know.

I'm not sure whether she was happy with what she got, but I feel rather smug to have been singled out for an interview. Not as eloquent as I could have been—still, my voice will be aired on the radio, heard by many.

RELAX, REACH, YOU
GOTTA BELIEVE

We felt righteous in our anger, our injustice seen and regarded as something worth people's time. A valuable argument to bring to the table. At times, it felt a bit like we were simply entertainers, performing for the crowd, playing an assigned role. The shades of skin were visible markers in the huge crowd, distinguishing between the entertainment and the onlookers.

I didn't mind, though. I held my head up high. I feel this was what I was born to do all along. I'm wearing my black turtleneck and Horace's red shoes. I've taken to putting my hair up in a bun with a purple velvet scrunchie; I just never get around to cutting it anymore. I'm glad Davinder can't see me like this, but I sure feel good right now. To think how scared I'd been last night; a tingling premonition, looming doom. Clearly, I had been wrong.

Our hearts are singing as we carry our signs and banners home, laying them to sleep beside our beds, lovingly, like small children who'd been particularly good all day. We are convinced that things are going to change. That the situation is most definitely looking up. This is just the first step, no?

At least, that's what Zhivago has been telling us over the past month.

What do we think happens next? What are our demands, our greater plans?

Well, I think most of us, we aren't even sure. Change. Fundamental all-around change. That was it.

I close my eyes and listen to our heartsong. Always about to escalate, it never reaches a proper peak. It just goes on and on and on. In the end, there are only drums.

FRANZ AND ODILE: WHY DON'T YOU CLOSE THE HOOD

ODILE: *Why don't you close the hood?*
FRANZ: *It doesn't close.*

Near the end of the movie, when Odile is still sullen and shaken from a heist gone magnificently wrong, she asks Franz to close the hood of the car.

It's all there, in his reply. You seek what, exactly? A home, a heart, protection from the dark? But the hood doesn't close; it's been broken since the first scene, the doors have been taken off of the hinges, there's only a sheath of foil between you and the elements; it's not a real gun, not a real house, and no real money, after all; being "safe" is an illusion, and all indicators of safety and its infrastructure (fences, walls, doors, suits of armor, meeting minutes, Europe, whatever, really, *whatever*) are illusionary. Of course they are, didn't you know? Merely Band-Aids for sore souls.

CATCHING SILVER CARP
IN BIRCH TREES

I dream I have to catch silver carp flying through a forest of skinny birch trees. The carp are fat Kashmiri carp. Flying isn't easy for them, for they are quite heavy. I've dreamed this dream before. The task is always the same. I have to rescue the fish and bring them back to the water. But whenever I reach the closest water source, for some reason an old sink in a forgotten house in the woods, and I turn on the tap for the water to run, the fish have already died. They gaze at me through blind eyes, silent and accusing.

Then, I have to eat them. No way around it. I have to swallow them whole like a hungry bear in a river when the salmon travel upstream. Sometimes I wake up sucking a lemon, or an eye. Thankfully, in my dreams, the carp are entirely boneless.

A scream?

I lift my head and turn around, half asleep. I can't see a thing. Inside the container is pitch-black.

The rest of the night is dreamless.

INTIMIDATIONS I

Someone has peed in our beds. Like, all of our blankets and sleeping bags—must have done it while we were at work in the tunnels.

Was it several men, or just one person, with an excessive amount of pee at his disposal? He must have drunk copious amounts of water beforehand.

INTIMIDATIONS II

Our shovels are gone. The black box is empty. When we ask where they've gone and what we should do about it, we're told, *Just use your hands then*. So we do.

INTIMIDATIONS III

We wake to find that the Caravan Kitchen has burned down. Burnt plastic smells disgusting.

IMAGINE IF IT WAS CONTAGIOUS

It is Arthur and Odile who finally sleep together; as we watch them slumber in embrace, we see there are marks of mold and damp on the wall, like the house has vitiligo. Imagine if it was contagious, infecting the whole movie roll, obliterating all: the love, the quest, the heist, the make-believe.

AND SO, WE BURN

Smoke, throat, scratch, constricted, eyes, a burning sensation; I cannot see a thing. Awake so fast I leave my consciousness behind. I try coming up for air, hurriedly, greedily. I get up, feeling around wildly, blindly, my feet get entangled in my blanket, I stumble, fall, hit the floor hard, *fuck, fuck*, incandescent pain, blood in my mouth.

Strong hands pull me outside, roughly; I am being dragged while half trying to crawl myself. My shoulder hits the metal frame of the door with full force; it will hurt for days to come. Outside, air, air, air, I cough, retch, vomit, a thin yellow fluid, and I spit out my tooth, a razor-sharp incisor, bloody upon the yellowed grass. I clutch my mouth, so much blood, get up onto my knees, and only now I see: fire. White, irate, blazing, hot fire. Container ONE is up in flames. The roof has been obliterated. My face feels like when I open the oven door and hot air erupts up my eyes. My lashes stick together like they've melted.

What the fuck? Harbir, what the fuck?

I—

Where is Zhiv?

Harbir?

Harbir doesn't look at me. He touches my arm, squeezes it briefly, and turns, running toward the watering hose, where they're all up at it already, Sukha and Tarsem filling buckets of water, buckets we normally use to transport new earth or fertilizer to feed the radish seedlings so they may flourish and grow.

CAKE

In the end, there is nothing left but a frisson of ash in the air. I imagine his body as it could have been, had I found it; untouched, intact.

I shift Zhivago's head onto my lap and put one hand on his forehead like I am feeling for a fever. And to maybe catch an essence of him while it's leaving his body. I lower my head toward his head. His forehead smells of cake. Milk and egg whites, lots of butter. Like a Russian doll, I can see all his former selves encapsulated in that forehead, being released one by one, forming a dancing roundelay around me while I hold his body. They are all wearing green dungarees, swinging cooking spoons and banners. They are laughing pearly little laughs; minuscule Zhivago laughs.

And then, just like that, they're gone. The milk has boiled over and evaporated. We had the fire on full and turned to leave the stove, just for a second—too long. All that's left is burned residue on the ground; hardened, solid, unmoving.

Light brown lips with a few dark dots scattered around the edges, slightly open, turning purple and blue—there are clots of earth in his mouth. I softly scoop them out with my fingers. Strange to feel his tongue, lying limp.

I let him slide off my knees placing his head softly in the dirt and I permit myself to slide with him.

NEVER TOGETHER

FRANZ: *Isn't it strange how people never form a whole?*

ODILE: *In what way?*

FRANZ: *They are never together. They remain separate. Each goes his own way.*

PART
FOUR
SCENDERE

THE COORDINATORS

The coordinators coordinate picket fences, international textile fairs, and shipping across the Mediterranean sea.

Coordinators coordinate the supply of flour and cocaine alike; they coordinate irregular flows of ideas and dangerous degrees of resistance. Coordinators coordinate the sound of music, the course of love, and global emergencies. Coordinators can very well coordinate world wars.

Coordinator is a beautiful job title, encompassing endless duties and possibilities. It sounds friendlier than manager, no? Also, you can pay a coordinator a little less than a manager, if you like. That is entirely up to you. Coordinators are essential. They are needed in your town, too. Possibly even in your very own household.

The coordinators can be found almost anywhere in the world; they take on different shapes and wear different shoes. Before the Italian coordinators, there were the Punjabi coordinators. In Jalandhar, the coordinators were called travel agents. Together, they form a big fat Coordinator-at-Large.

The coordinators are tools in a huge global toolbox; heavy to lift, and no one can be bothered to take a proper look inside. It's been around for so long, that big rusty thing. You cannot open it without exhausting yourself, and the lid keeps getting stuck.

PECORE NERE

The black sheep are thinking

Soft vibrations

bellies like clouds

I want to get lost in your curls.

Dusty, wiry, hardboiled, lucky curls.

I am not sure whether I am protecting you, or you are protecting me.

Pecore nere—I am your cattle, your humble servant. A guardian, but no more.

I wish you could meet your distant cousins, the Punjabi goats with hanging ears. They are droll indeed. They may look like village idiots to you, the whole lot of them, but they are agile and cunning.

It's merely a trick, an inside joke: that idiotic smile.

HAPPY TV: SUNSET DANCE II

A boy dances underneath a gulmohar tree in rural Punjab, by the side of a dusty village road broad enough for tractors. His hair falls in a funny way. He is wearing a bright orange shirt and purple pants. He has taken off his shoes. The soles of his feet are red from the rotting blossoms.

A "Sunset Dance I" implies the existence of a "Sunset Dance II."

I press record.

I take myself in my own hands, presenting myself to the camera.

I don't smile. My mouth is tired. My shoulder blades won't allow me to move as I used to. I shake out my legs, jog on the spot. I roll my tongue and roar like a lion. The sound is small.

I begin my dance. I am washing my hair in the well with my brothers. Rubbing my head, kneading my scalp. Then I wash my whole body, squeezing it clean from all I have seen; it's a tough job. I need to scrub thoroughly, my limbs, my arms, my fingertips. I shake my head to dry the wet strands. I get down on all fours, like a dog after a bath in the river, arching my spine and offering my ass. Then I am Ambika, rising in defense, straightening her spine to throw the world a look like a bullet. I elevate myself, up to the great storage ceiling, where a lightbulb and a rock are swaying in close embrace. In the end, I crouch down to the earth, pressing my hands together as if in prayer.

For a brief moment, I exist in a blank space: a white cube smelling of lemony cleaning agent. Time expands and contracts.

I could be a cloud of cotton candy, a gulmohar tree, a bag, a pack of flour, a tiny shovel, or a pearl on a necklace in Punjab, either side.

Then, I fall into the earth. She envelopes me soft and wormy, and my head becomes a cabbage, glorious and ripe, which Europe harvests effortlessly off my neck. She carries it up to her fat cloud and roasts it in an oven overnight; the outer leaves turn black but inside it gets sweet and juicy.

Franz and Odile sit in a car just outside Paris; it has broken down along the peripheral motorway. They are baking sugar rotis on a camping cooker. How did they learn to do that? Syrup is dripping onto the tawa; sweet smoke is filling the car. Odile is rubbing her hands in anticipation. I can feel the saliva accumulating in her mouth like it is my own.

Sylvester Stallone is running up a Sardinian hill. At the top, Zhivago is dressed in an embroidered blue salwar kameez, moving his hands. I recognize the gestures. I think he is dancing.

Finally, Zhivago turns into my mother, Gul, remote control in hand. Her eyes are small, tired, and red. She exhales audibly and switches off the TV.

CONTAIN YOURSELF

When is space? Where is time, really?

Events are condensing, then building up rapidly, a fast-rising soufflé. But when you open the door of the oven, it deflates, *shoo*, just like that, collapsing into a flat amorphous shape. Oh no. Quel dommage!

There is hope still. We can reuse the ingredients; adapt and transform. We are good at that, aren't we? Making it work. We are empathic, flexible, and resilient.

Hard to tell apart beginnings and endings. Trying to contain things while containing oneself. Fetching the right words and repressing the wrong ones. Same, same.

I, for my part, am never sure what will come out of my mouth.

IMAGINE IF THIS
WAS CONTAGIOUS

Imagine if this was contagious. Imagine if it was true.

Imagine if I swallowed all those smooth pale stones.

They would make me very heavy. I would sink quickly, for sure.

I let the stones be stones. They will still lie in the river when I return to it. I will be a different person, but the stones will be the same.

My phone is dead. The research has come to an end. As of yet, we are unsure of the outcome. The big machine is processing, still.

FATEHPAL: STILL ACTIVE

Happy, how are you? Can't reach you . . .
Hey! How are you doing, brother?
Did you find a girl at last? Eloping? ;-) You can tell me.
Is this number still active?

MY MOUTH IS A PORTAL

My mouth is a portal, living and moist.
    I swallow you gently.
    You can lie on my tongue, quite comfortably.
    I will keep you safe; you can travel along as long as you like.

YOU SURROUND ME

Still, you surround me. You surround me like sweet liqueur surrounds
a floating cherry.

CELINA BALJEET BASRA

FONTANA DI TREVI, AGAIN

I haven't been this naked in quite a while. I am freezing my ass off. How does it look by the way? My ass.

The fountain is wide open today. An open invitation. To take a bath.

With Neptune, the ultimate hunk, looking on.

Come here! he says. And: *It's OK to make mistakes. We all do!*

I put my head against the cool wall and once again swallow that big scream I've been saving for a special occasion.

Carefully, sitting down first, lowering my feet one by one. The ground beneath my toes feels gooey. The water is cold, green, foul, reaching only to my calves. But I want a proper bath, don't I? I get down on my knees. Press my head underwater and open my eyes. And then I push out a scream so huge, it shakes the ground of the fountain, making the euro coins vibrate like an orchestra of copper-covered steel and Nordic gold. I shake the very foundations of Rome, built by demigods, raised by a she-wolf.

Bubbles escape my mouth, dancing through the rotten water. I resurface, catching my breath. I open my palms and let hand-fuls of water run over my head, like I've seen people do in the Ganges.

I start gathering handfuls of coins, donated to the water spirits in abundance, giggling. Now that I've started, I can't stop: giggling, that is. I have nowhere to put the coins, so I put a few in my mouth and let the rest glide back into the water. I bash the water with my hands like a child in a bubble bath. I am creating waves and foam and glory. The coins are sitting uncomfortably in my throat. But once you make a decision, see it through. So I swallow. It's not as hard as you might think; saliva is a useful lubricant.

I feel my stomach rumble. I cough up a coppery sound. The rumbling grows into a commotion, a revolution, a full-on emergency diarrhea situation. My body is rejecting Europe itself. All that I've ingested since my arrival: that first nervous espresso, the tiny creamy dolce, the Montanaras, the fried fish, spaghetti vongole, my first sip of red wine, a dessert tasting of raisins and rum, the expired tinned food, a frozen pizza melted in the sun, Zhivago's Surinamese chicken sandwich—out, out, everything must go.

I eject all the things I never said. Every word I swallowed before it saw the light of day. Every utterance in my mother tongue that no one could possibly understand.

EUROPE: OOO

Thank you for your message. I am out of the office from May 1 and will have limited email access while I am away. If you need immediate assistance, please contact the Chair of the Committee of Irregular Arrivals at talmon-dunkelberg@ep.europa.eu. Otherwise, I will respond to your email when I return.

Sincerely,
Europe
europe@europa.eu
Head Recruitor
Department of Irregular Arrivals
Department of Border Control and Insulation

MON HISTOIRE SE FINIT LÀ.

Comme dans un roman bon marché.
À ce moment sublime de l'existence où rien ne déclin.

EPILOGUE

HARBIR

Happy was found in Rome, in front of a supermarket as they opened shop. They think he'd stopped breathing in the early hours of the morning. Didn't have a passport or any documents on him. But they found my number—I was the last person he'd called. I got in touch with his brother Fatehpal, who drove down to Italy in an old Renault 100. The car broke down on the way to Rome. It's still stranded there, in the middle of nowhere. At some point, some teenagers set it on fire. Ashes are fertile; now it's covered in grass and mirto bushes, and foxes have taken it over as a den.

Apparently, Zhivago had been involved in this kind of thing before, on other farms. Blood oranges, pomelos, and unseasonal raspberries. He went around and incited riots. Slowly and steadily infusing the workers' minds with thoughts of rebellion. Organizing protests, demanding minimum wage and humane living conditions.

Happy was convinced Zhiv's death was his fault. Guilt is a gnarly worm. It eats you up entirely.

What's that? Oh, yeah. True. He'd been obsessed with pecore nere, ever since I first told him about my acquaintance in Sardegna. Reading up on their history, their breeding and welfare, scribbling in his notebook. He even gave me that cover letter to send to Hari Singh. I never mailed it, though. I kept the letter. It made me laugh. What he wrote was true, in a lot of ways.

I own a market stall in Bibbiena now. Import business. Textiles— socks, comfortable underwear and such. One hundred percent cotton, Lycra, elastic. Here's my card. Sometimes, I still do car repairs on the side.

My wife, Choti, came over, too, and she gave birth to two girls. Twins! Look, here: Sunny, Sunny Paramveer Kaur—and this is little Gioia Karamveer Kaur. You can't tell them apart, can you? Lots of hair, yes! And big ears, to listen and learn. We have our hands full.

It's all properly arranged. This is my passport. Freshly printed. Maybe one day we will return. For now, we will stay. Our house is a small and crumbling one, out near Poppi, new repairs every day, had to retile the kitchen floor by hand after a water damage—but it is our own.

I finally bought a Fiat Panda. Il Zero, bright red, designed by Giorgetto Giugiaro and Aldo Mantovani. I know: I'm too big a man for such a small car. And my turban—I have to take it off when I drive, as the ceiling is too low. I think of Happy whenever I wear my hair up in a bun.

When driving, I always turn up the music as loud as I can. You wouldn't know this by looking at me, but I always sing along. I know all the words, and my voice is a fine baritone.

ROSELLA

Happy's head was resting on a bag when they found him, an old-fashioned leather bag, carrying his essential items. It contained an empty bottle of Amla hair oil, a small painting of two lovers riding on a fish, a glossy brochure from a theme park called Wonderland, and nine notebooks, scribbled with tall, slanted handwriting. They were filled with notes, songs, poems, half-written screenplays, conversations with imaginary people, and several fragments of a novel, but never more than a few pages of hopeful beginnings.

We'd never exchanged numbers, and, for a long time, we didn't know what happened to him. But Bogdan knows someone at the radish farm. We heard he disappeared after one of his fellow workers had died. Looking back, Bo thinks he might've seen Happy sleeping in front of a supermarket once, late at night; but he's not sure if it was him.

When he died, Happy was wearing track pants and Horace's black turtleneck.

FATEHPAL

The retrieval of the body—hard to call it that. Hard to ignore the calls from Gul, too, for days on end, because I didn't know what to tell her. That there once was a boy called Happy, and now, there was only a body to retrieve.

Why did no one call an ambulance? I don't know. Maybe he was alone?

Why did you not check on him? Because I didn't find the time. Because I wanted to believe that all was well.

The repatriation process—I had no idea how. Don't speak a word of Italian. I checked the list provided on lastjourney.in and, after a lot of difficulty, obtained the necessary documents: death certificate, consular report. I arranged to embalm the body, organized a coffin box and a protective wrap. I booked his flight to Delhi, as well as mine.

I cried all the way from Hannover to the Alps.

What was that song I used to sing?

Fly up, Happy, fly up high, your brother loves you, your sister loves you, the crows they fly, they will be here forever, and so will you, and so will you, and so will you.

ZHIVAGO

Happy smelled like barfi, wet earth, and fish fry. Hard to think these odors could harmonize, but they did. His hands were constantly in his hair, trying to get it out of his eyes. He had trustworthy hands. Honest hands. His eyes could very well pretend, but his hands never could. They stuck to childlike habits, grabbing and feeling things. They were made to touch and be touched.

Happy couldn't tell a story in a straightforward manner. He got sidetracked and loopholed and exhausted himself on the way. Like a squirrel, he ran through the forest that was his own mind, digging up the whimsical, the chimerical, putting it in his flexible cheek pouches to store for later use. Sometimes, those pouches exploded, and he told you everything all at once. No need to keep track, just immerse yourself.

It was the small things. The things he got teased for. His gift for illusion. A flowery blanket, the questions he asked, the way he looked at me when I spoke. He turned a space into a room, and a room into a home. Happy didn't need rescuing, really. He had been free all along.

I did look into the mythology of the Indian Bird of Death. It is possible that eagle owls were the origin of the image; appearing at dawn, connecting night and day, life and death. Another real-life model could very well be the Sri Lankan frogmouth bird. When alarmed, it positions its body so that it can easily be mistaken for a jagged, broken branch. The bird opens its frog-like mouth wide when facing a threat; wide enough to swallow an entire soul, easily. Though, if Happy's soul was carried away from Italy, I think it must have been brought back by a Punjabi crow. The only one fit for the job. Crossing borders effortlessly to return him home, flapping her wings respectfully and laying him down by the old gulmohar tree.

The end was a minuscule glob of blood. Curdling in silence, clotting and plotting, ever since he'd hit his head back in Wonderland. Cutting off the circulation to Happy's brain. He was given extra time: a lot of whirling about in the kettle. A blaze, the birth of a crust, a surge of syrup in between. And the oil at the bottom was the color of the sun.

LIST OF ILLUSTRATIONS

ACKNOWLEDGMENTS

To Nila, for bestowing rhythm, energy, and love in abundance. To Björn, for your beautiful mind, for supporting my writing from the moment we met, for taking care.

Thanks to my family, for the stories, the love, and the fury. To Annika Rani, fellow escapist, and my mother, who gave me books and words, for which I am forever thankful. To Sophia Cara, whose energetic spirit is unmatched—and to my father, for aloo pakoras, and the fable of the crow and the water. (I think Aesop might have stolen it from a village in Punjab.)

Forever grateful to the amazing Alexander Reubert for reading that one page—the book wouldn't have happened without you.

Endlessly thankful for Deborah Ghim's brilliant mind; you are a genius, and the best shepherdess *Happy* could have wished for. Thanks also to Signe Swanson and all the wonderful people at Astra House involved in the making of this book.

Thank you to Ambika Thompson, and the lovely people in your workshops, for providing a safe space to write.

Thank you to Lea, the forever traveler, for her love for Fiat Pandas (named after the Roman goddess of travelers, Empanda).

Thank you to Jatinder Singh Durhailay and Johanna Tagada, whose beautiful wedding invitation, painted by Jatinder, I looked at for Babbu's fictional painting—the Bruce Lee portrait stuck into Davinder's mirror is inspired by one of Jatinder's works, too.

Thank you to Zhivago Holwijn, the anthropologist who kindly gave his name and his mother's recipe for Surinamese chicken sandwich.

And thank you to Nancy Adajania for introducing me to the split necklace of Mohenjo-daro during her workshop at Kochi Biennale.

Lastly, thanks to brilliant Alex Merto for giving this novel a face. :)

The Lost Interview with Bruce Lee departs from his interview with Pierre Berton (Pierre Berton Show, December 9, 1971), taking some liberties. The wisdoms of Guru Nanak are based on quotes from the Sri Guru Granth Sahib.

I am writing about a pigment in a Pietà by Giovanni Bellini, which is not in Rome but Berlin at the Gemäldegalerie.

Early in the novel, Happy tries to make sense of a nineteenth-century engraving that represents Europe and America as two women, their whiteness set off against the brown skin of a man seen crouched down, reading in the background. The choice to render America in the style of European neoclassicism, as a white woman crowned with a Native headdress, serves to distance her from "savage" Native Americans and enslaved African Americans and to reinforce colonial rule; important to keep in mind while you are looking at the image.

I know I can never truly walk in Happy's shoes. Even if the novel's entire cast and all its locations are entirely fictional, the underlying facts are very real. If Happy and his fellow farm workers had been successful in their uprising, maybe they would have gone on to found an initiative like Barikamà (*resilience*), a cooperative initiated by Suleiman Diara and a group of Malinese farmers in Italy, who left exploitative working conditions to produce and sell their own excellent yogurt and various vegetables; you can find them in several markets in Rome and elsewhere.

ABOUT THE AUTHOR

CELINA BALJEET BASRA is a writer and cultural worker based in Berlin. She is a founder of the Department of Love, a curatorial collective. *Happy* is her first novel.